Mariam's Wedding Gift and Other Offerings

Louise Thunin-Domaratius

Mariam's Wedding Gift and Other Offerings
Published through Lulu Enterprises, Inc.

Interior Book Design and Layout by
www.integrativeink.com

ISBN: 978-1-84799-312-0

The following stories have previously been published:
The Definition of a Russian String Quartet (in *New York Stories*)
Olive in Two Languages (in *Out of Line*)
Rummage Sale (in *Full Circle: A Journal of Poetry and Prose*)
Mirror (in *Fiction International*)
Big Top (in *Divide*/ also in *Pharos*, Paris, in different form)
Mariam's Wedding Gift (in *Fiction International*)
Blows to the Heart (in *Silent Voices*)

Mariam's Wedding Gift and Other Offerings was awarded an Honorable Mention in the Starcherone Fiction Prize competition, 2005

By the same author:

Gadji Quality Words in Print
Writing the Book of Ester, Quality Words in Print
Chats with Le Chat Gourmet (with Susan Marx), Lulu
La Nokriyah, Amalthée, France

Contents

THE DEFINITION OF A RUSSIAN STRING QUARTET

My gaze travelled upward from the first row where I was sitting, and, inevitably, the first thing I saw were his shoes. They were worn and dirty, not at all the shoes you expect on a concert musician. They ought to have been black patent leather, winking like twin mirrors, and here they were with the dust of miles on them and the scuff marks of history. Even the laces were exhausted, with lighter-colored extensions knotted on. I looked farther. The socks were acceptable, black and tight fitting, almost elegance itself as socks go, and the black suit could pass muster, lustered by use but not indecently shiny. The white shirt looked as if it had frequented the proper washing powders. The bow tie was just a wee bit rakishly askew, but that lent a boyish charm to his otherwise grave, worried expression. He wasn't used to these Western audiences, these grinning, Colgate-toothed Americans. He didn't know it was all right to smile.

The four shared a glance that could have been complicity or just a convention among them: Now we begin. Sasha (I learned later that he was called Sasha) dug his bow into the first bars of Koechel number 156 in G and a minuscule cloud of white rosin dust rose from the frog of his bow. The notes ran after one another like kittens at play, and, each time it was up to Sasha to take the initiative, his dark eyebrows came together, making a little furrowed place between them, while his black eyes sought the stocky cellist's opposite. His shoulders lurched forward, and the violin in his hands coughed out or sang out or wept so sweetly, that its voice, disembodied from the small wooden box, hung in the air above the chords and rhythms of the three other instruments with the grace and insistence of a siren's. One forgot the shoes. They were a mistake; everything in Sasha was aerial and translucent. There was no room for dust in his Mozart.

When it was over, the four of them stood shyly, their instruments against their chests, and endured the applause. Their faces were closed and passive, not proud or even determined like the bronze proletarian heroes' in the Moscow subway. When will these musicians from behind the fallen iron curtain learn to lighten up, I wondered. I wished I had a rose with me to toss onto the stage, as they do over there. Then, perhaps he would have smiled at me.

I had my note pad with me at the ready. If I was a failed violinist, I wasn't so bad as a music critic, and tonight's assignment was the Vaslav Quartet: Mozart, Dvorak and Borodin. The Mozart was studious and then jocular, the Dvorak a Bohemian's wink at the new world, but the Borodin was sheer luminosity. He and we are of one piece, they seemed to tell us, and our souls wear the same landscape of steppe and snow and rolling Volga. I slipped backstage for my interview. I could speak Russian; that was how I got to do all the Russian recitals and concerts that came to our area. And come they did, now that the wall was down, and exit visas could be had, and profiteering impresarios hovered over the feast, forgetting, alas, to feed the musicians more often than not.

Sasha's long, brown hair was tied in the back in a tail Wolfgang Amadeus would have frowned on as unnecessarily long. His companions were more seriously classical: Vladimir, viola, balding; Nicolaï, second violin, with a shock of gray frizz over his forehead; Lev, cello, as spherical and blond as the wheat bushels of the Ukraine.

They all had First Prizes from the Tchaikovsky Conservatory, they said. It had been a long time since they had earned a decent living with their instruments, and even this metropolitan tour would probably not bring enough to keep them in vodka.

I offered a drink at my place. Vladimir crushed his cigarette underfoot and said he had to get back to the hotel. Nicolaï and Lev needed time to write home. Sasha looked at me sideways and said why not. I hadn't counted on just one, but if this one had as winning a way with a woman as he did with a violin, the part might be worth the sight-reading. I figured I was a big girl and could look out for myself.

« What's the definition of a Russian string quartet? » Sasha asked, as we walked from the backstage entrance to my car in the parking lot.

I said I gave up.

« A Russian symphony orchestra on tour abroad. »

I laughed, thinking he meant that four musicians were all the State could afford to send. Later, I wondered if it meant the others had all defected. I'm still not sure. Had he missed a word or two in English?

We drove from the school auditorium where the quartet had played that evening to my square, three-storey brick apartment building. It stands on the corner of an otherwise ordinary, lower-middle class suburban street not far from the train station. The street is complete with lawns and trees and clapboard houses of pastel colors or plain white.

« Have you seen other American homes? » I asked Sasha. He said no, they had just come over a week ago, and, indeed, his eyes drank in everything like an eager child's at the zoo.

Outdoors, spring in New Jersey streets smells poignantly of freshly-mown grass. The fragrance lingers even in the evening. Inside, the floorboards of my 1950s apartment, warmed by sunlight during the day, exhale their own woody sweetness and promise of summer heat to come. There is no elevator at 56 Schoolhouse Street; the three flights are easy to negotiate and the landings scrupulously clean. Not planning on company, I hadn't tidied anything, but my place is basically presentable, and I am quite proud of it. Sasha took in the love seat with its jumble of patchwork cushions, the glass coffee table where my mug still sat, my desk with the computer screen lit up, the bookshelves draped with trailing ivy plants, and my favorite prints, posters, and foreign calendars on the wall.

« This place is all for you alone? » he asked.

« Yes, » I said, pointing out that I also had a bedroom, kitchen, full bathroom. He said no more, and I supposed he was thinking a family of four would be happy to have that much space where he came from.

He noticed my antique wooden music stand in the corner with the *Meditation* from *Thaïs* on it for show. It was the only piece I had ever successfully memorized. « You play...? »

« Seven years of violin lessons, » I said. « And I can hardly say so. But I do wish I could. You...uh, you give lessons, perhaps? »

He shrugged. « I could. You'd have to practice. »

« Naturally! »

He looked at me curiously. « Show me what you know! »

« What about the vodka? »

« The vodka too. With pleasure. »

He took the little glass reverently in his hands and looked at me. He wanted to see my violin. I lifted it from the plush and unwound the old flower-print scarf that swathed its warm, cherry-colored body. Sasha pressed his nose against the « f » holes and breathed deeply. Then he held its satiny curves at a distance and admired the handiwork. « Very fine. This is an American violin? »

« Italian. Contemporary. It's a Rosadoni. A man from Como. It was a present from my parents, who hoped for more. I call it ' Rosi.' I guess that's silly, but it's like a person to me. »

« And the tone? »

« Try it for yourself! »

He attached the shoulder pad, tightened the bow and tuned the four strings. Then he shut his eyes and began with *Thaïs*. My poor, orphaned instrument had finally found a home.

« Your neighbors maybe are trying to sleep? »

« They might be, » I admitted. « Or, if they're awake, they'll be marveling at the progress I've made. »

« Let me just see if your position is correct, » Sasha said, and I obediently set the violin under my chin and lifted my left arm. From behind me, he gently adjusted the curve of my left hand over the fingerboard.

« With your permission, » he said, amused, touching my fingers with his own slender ones. « And you mustn't hang onto your bow for dear life that way. Relax! Supple, the muscles! » He held my right hand gently and shook it. His black eyes were laughing at me.

« I thought Russians were mostly blond, » I said. « Where did you get those almond eyes? »

« I'm part Tatar, » he said. « And Jewish and Gypsy. The last two ingredients make the best violinists. »

He was so close to me, I could smell the freshly-laundered cotton of his dress shirt.

« I think you'll be a good student, » he added.

I said I would try.

He wouldn't let me drive him to his little hotel in the town center but said he had to walk, to take in as much of suburban New Jersey as he could. They would be leaving for New York and a series of gigs in a couple of days. The city was only half an hour's train ride away. He would be back, and I had better start by reviewing Sevcik.

Sasha used « Rosi » now in concert. His Soviet-period fiddle was a cigar-box, he said, but the violin that vibrated the best to his touch was my own body. He gave me lessons in more than music during his American April. Scales before the music stand, others in my small summery-smelling bedroom, and the compliance of my bowing muscles seemed directly proportionate to the degree of pleasure that preceded.

He wouldn't call me Kathy with that impossible « th » in the middle but every manner of Russian diminutive from Katia to Katinka to Katiusha. I felt I belonged in the meanders of Dostoevsky or Tolstoy, where the characters appear to change names every few pages. His was Alexander Petrovich Ivanov, but the third syllable, the « sand » of his first name, made « Sasha. » He wouldn't tell me much about what he had done at home other than describe the fight for your life that a conservatory prize means in Moscow.

On the slightly beaten photograph in his wallet, the ash-blond woman with the broad, Slavic cheek-bones was, he said, his sister, Irina. The two children were his niece and nephew, Tania and Kostia.

« There's no resemblance between you and Irina, » I protested.

« She's not a natural blond, » was all he said.

« But the children look a little like you. Those oblique eyes.»

He shrugged.

« Why don't we see Irina's husband? »

« He was behind the camera. »

I believed him because I wanted to, but the picture haunted me.

ஒ

Midsummer in lower Manhattan. The little park where the concert was to be held was already filled with sound: bugs hidden in the foliage, indefatigably scraping the tiny bows of their outer wings, children running after a half-deflated beachball in a far corner, the hum and occasional honking of traffic passing on the street beyond the heavy curtain of trees. Ears shut, you could believe you were in a world apart, but open them again, and the city filtered back to you, playing its own chaotic, buzzing song. The black, sun-soaked asphalt underfoot warmed the soles of your sandals, and the sun took forever to lower its hot, weary body beneath the line of the trees. Nicolaï, Vladimir, Lev, and Sasha, instruments in hand, passed by the slatted wooden chair where I sat at the edge of the front row, bowed crisply and took their places on the four waiting seats. New York temperatures had made them drop ties and jackets, and the collars of their white shirts were informally open. Their shoes were new.

That meaningful glance again, and Borodin soared toward the treetops, meeting the final sun rays and a pigeon as it took off, wings beating black against the backdrop of gray, humid sky.

« I know a French place, a bistro in the East Village, » I said.

They nodded; they had funds now, and, after the exhilaration of applause, an anonymous hotel room would be a let-down. Night stuck to our skins like damp, black velvet.

Over a sweating, balloon-shaped glass of cool, dry white wine, Lev extracted from his pocket one of those funny, Soviet-style envelopes with *kuda* (where to) and *komu* (to whom) printed near the top, right under the stamp, with more lines directly underneath for the name and address of the sender. He drew two shiny identity photos from it, two fair, moon-faced children, boy and girl.

« God, how I miss them, » he said, mopping his forehead. « Nastia's taken first prize for her level in harp this year at the Academy, and Grigory begins the bass viol in the fall. » The little girl wore a huge, blue bow cocked on one side of her blond bowl-cut. I thought Grigory looked a bit young and defenseless to be confronting a bass viol.

« What pictures have *you* to show us? » I asked Sasha a bit coyly, I have to admit, but his look was unfathomable, unconcerned.

« No one writes me, » he said. « I haven't the luck of my cohorts. »

Nicolaï and Vladimir exhanged glances. At any rate, I thought they exchanged glances. That they were meaningful ones is more than I could vouch for.

Sasha returned to New Jersey with me on the last train. The air-conditioning was turned up too high, and I shivered next to him. He didn't put his arm around me, and that was when I started to nag him. About his life in Russia. Past girl-friends. His niece and nephew. I tried to avoid the name of Irina, but it wormed its way in like a wiggling belly-dancer between the lines the New Jersey Transit posted obsessively in front of us in bright green, electronic lettering.

Be considerate of other riders. Speak softly.

« Sasha, » I whispered, « how many women have you had? »

« Katia, my heart, why do Americans always think in terms of quantity? »

« I'm sorry. »

Please keep feet off seats.

Someone's cell phone tootled its four-note jingle across the aisle. « Hey, Edie, would you believe it, I got three answers to my ad, » a man's voice answered. « I met the first one last night. »

Edie must have said something; there was a pause.

« ...She owns her house, has an Alfa Romeo. But listen, this is just between you and I... » His voice filled the entire, sleepy train car. The *you and I* made me wince. « *Physically*, she's not my type. »

Two passengers opposite smirked.

Save money, buy monthly tickets.

« Does Irina work? » I couldn't help myself.

The conductor reached us and snapped with swift, rabid hand at our strip-like tickets with his puncher, making holes in an enigmatic myriad of places. His wrist movements were as deft as

Sasha's. Occupational hazard: tendinitis, I couldn't help thinking. I hoped he wasn't an amateur musician.

« My sister?, » Sasha replied. « Yes, she's a salesgirl. »

Nothing more.

« And your brother-in-law? »

He frowned slightly. « You're from the CIA, *milaïa*, maybe? »

Do not ride in the vestibule.

« Oh, Sasha, I just want to know about *you*, about your life... »

Suddenly he noticed the goose bumps on my bare arms and put his new jacket over the front of my light summer dress. « No sense of nuance in this place. » He shook his head. « Where are the dynamics? Hot as hell or cold as the North Pole. Same for everything else. »

I felt cowed. I huddled behind the dark worsted.

Never get on or off a moving train.

He glanced up at the panel. « And they take people for bumbling idiots. Unless it's that they're afraid of lawsuits. For not warning you or something. »

I held my tongue. I simply noticed how his complexion had gone from eastern European pasty to healthy American tan on a good diet of fresh fruit and vegetables, red meat and fish, how handsome he looked in his new clothes, remembered how miraculous he sounded when he played my Rosadoni. He *must* love it here. He had to.

In the middle of the night the telephone rang. Is there anything more frightening than a telephone that startles you out of quiet sleep? Only urgent, bad news comes at night. Or, with luck, wrong numbers.

« Hello? » I forced out a small, scratchy voice, my heart pounding, and a flood of apologetic Russian came from the other end. The connection was clear. I would have thought one of the other quartet members was calling, except that I was hearing a woman's voice. « *Minutochka*, » I said. I handed the receiver to Sasha.

I heard him say « *Slushaï, Ira!* » several times, and a chill raised the light down on my forearms despite the hot summer night.

He was speaking to Irina. The whirring of the little electric fan blotted out most of it from me.

Sasha hated air conditioning: « phoney, canned atmosphere, » he said. « Fake settings here, fake sophistication, even fake air. » When he had placed the phone back in its wall cradle, he immediately started pulling on trousers, shirt, socks, and shoes.

« You're leaving? »

He kissed me. « My sister needs me. It's urgent, Katiusha. I'm sorry. I want to get the first plane. »

« But what about your concert dates? »

« The others will figure something out. »

« Is she ill? Hurt? »

« No, no, nothing like that. Too long to explain. Can I use your phone to call a taxi? »

« Sasha, you can use anything of mine. »

I heard him ask to be driven to Kennedy. A hundred dollars' worth of taxi. Did he realize that? He must have been in a hurry indeed.

In his haste, Sasha had grabbed a violin, his own. « Rosi, » in its black, professional-looking, rectangular case, sulked in a corner of the room, not far from the ashtray that held Sasha's cigarette butts. Everyone smoked in Russia, Sasha had told me.

« And the life expectancy is only about sixty for men, » I'd added, a tad self-righteous.

« Life expectancy also means you expect something *from* life, » he'd said. « When you haven't got that, you live for the present moment. You smoke, you drink, and, if you're lucky, you forget. »

With all my heart I hoped he had found something to expect here. Although I hated the smell of cold tobacco, I took a butt and put it between my lips. It was all that was left to me now of Sasha.

Five days passed and still Sasha did not call. His companions billed themselves the Novgorod Chamber Ensemble, and their repertoire changed. Ex-Soviet quartet down now to ex-Soviet trio, I thought ruefully. They'd found a pianist through some underground channel that secretes Russian musicians on demand, and tonight there would be Beethoven's Archduke. Vladimir, the violist, would sit that one out. I was next to him, my question burning in my mind, keeping me from listening. The exquisite yearnings of the *poco piu adagio* wafted past me, background music to some other world.

After the concert, they smiled at me, comprehending my dismay but saying nothing.

« He called you? » I finally asked.

Lev nodded yes.

« He had to go back for Irina? »

« Yes, for Irina's sake. She needed him. »

I thought Lev looked chagrined.

« His wife, Irina, is that it? And no one wants to tell me? » I felt wretched and abandoned and imagined they were feeling sorry for me.

Nicolaï's gray eyebrows lifted. « Sasha hasn't got a wife, » he said. « Is that what you thought? That Irina was his wife? That he was lying to you about her? »

« Yes. » Tears rose to my eyes in spite of myself. I felt ashamed and foolish.

« Tell her. It won't hurt, » Lev said.

« Irina's husband is something of a petty Mafia member, » Nicolaï said, his voice quiet.

I felt inundated with relief. The problem was elsewhere. It wasn't with Sasha, with another woman. Irina's husband could have been king of the dons for all I cared.

« He got himself into a nasty lot of trouble these past few days. Stole the car of a high functionary, then had an accident with it. He smashed it up all by himself, no other casualties. »

« Was he killed? » I ventured.

« No, but he was badly messed up. Got away from the scene of the accident all right, but he collapsed later. Irina thought there was internal bleeding when she called Sasha that night. »

« Why didn't she just call a doctor? An ambulance? »

« Because they'd have figured it out, that he was the one. Prison terms are long and harsh in our country, Kathy. » He pronounced it Kat-sea. « And if they'd realized he was the culprit, then they probably wouldn't have gone too far out of their way to get him medical aid anyway. »

« Good Lord, but he has children. »

« No mortal good to them in prison, Kat-sea. »

« Do you know if he's still alive? If Sasha will be back? »

« No. » They looked embarrassed, as if somehow it was their fault I'd lost Sasha.

« He'll probably call you soon, or write you. When this blows over. »

« Yes, soon. I'm sure, » I said. My voice quavered, and I was sure of nothing at all.

I would take « Rosi » out of its case and stroke its varnish. I sought some vibration left over from Sasha's fingertips on the ebony fingerboard, but for me, the bow would only elicit wails. I pressed my left cheek into the hollow of the chin rest and tried to imagine it was his shoulder I felt, horizontal and slightly bony. Then I would put the instrument back to bed in the sturdy, coffin-like box, rubbing the excess rosin from the strings below the bridge with a little square of ancient cotton, soft as silk from wear.

Time passed, but none of us heard anything from Sasha. The ringing of the phone rebounded against the walls of his empty flat, and no one knew where Irina lived. I covered a series of piano recitals and found them despicable. Pounders, they were, those pianists, hammering, vengeful beings. Chopin and Liszt gave me headaches.

Then one day the kitschy Russian envelope was for me. The flimsy paper was decorated on the left with the naïve print of a tabby cat, complete with pink ribbon around its neck. « The European short-hair »: I deciphered the capital Cyrillic letters. On the right were the two storeys of names and addresses, mine, then his beneath. I willed myself not to open it before I was upstairs, before I had shut the door behind me. I made myself wait, because as long as I waited, I could continue to hope, hope to find inside the date of his return. I scanned the Cyrillic, but no dates caught my eye. I sat down. I would read it syllable by foreign syllable, in order.

My Katiusha, it began. That was my favorite nickname, the same one as in the folk song about the girl who waits for her beloved soldier beneath the flowering pear and apple trees. First he explained about Irina, about how dreadful it had been for her to lose her husband, to see him wither and die before her own, helpless eyes, like a plant under a curse. The doctor had written « heart failure » on the death certificate. She had paid him not to probe too deeply. The children had been devastated, and they clung to Sasha.

I was filled with horror, reading this. He would come back to me, I was sure now. His country was full of inhumanity and corruption. He knew that, didn't he? I read on:

And now, Katiusha, as summer draws to an end, the woods are filled with the sweetest smelling loam ever, and we go early in the morning with large wicker baskets on our arms. When we come home, the sun is hot and our baskets are filled. Irina cooks the mushrooms and fills enough jars with them for the entire winter. She is putting up purple plums now, too, and the other day the whole simmering copper pot of them boiled over. The violet carpet in front of the stove was fine enough for a bishop, but rather a sticky mess to clean up. Never fear, the plums are plentiful, and we will have compote galore.

I saw the most beautiful fur chapka for you at the marketplace this morning. They sell them for about eighty of your dollars, but if you bargain astutely, you can do better than that. My Katiusha, when will you come to me? I miss you; I miss holding you in my arms. I have thought about nothing else since I had to leave you so suddenly. I have classes now at the local music school and private lessons for a few who can afford them. Believe it or not, I even give private English lessons. My pupils are so impressed with my « American » accent! When you come, I feel sure we can get you a teaching position at the normal school here. They do so need to train teachers of English...

Tears welled in my eyes. Not once did he mention returning to America. Only loam and mushrooms and purple plums. And for me, that would be...what, exactly? Fragrant, freshly-cut grass, autumn leaves crisp underfoot or burning in small, pungent pyres, cinnamon-spiced cider and doughnuts? I could make a long list. I even thought to reach for a piece of paper. As I did, my gaze rested on « Rosi, » docile and mute in its corner.

I lugged my violin in its elaborate wrapping to the post-office. I asked about insurance, filled in all the forms. In our little town, packages to Russia are rare; I caused quite a stir among the personnel.

Once everything was worked out, and « Rosi » was on its cosmopolitan way, from Italy to America to Russia, I walked the few blocks to catch the Manhattan train. A wind quintette from Tbilissi was playing that evening, and I was to do the review. I lifted my eyes to the unavoidable electronic panel at the end of the car, to its crystalline, green announcement :

Last station - New York Penn I read.

Big Top

« Le seul compliment qui me fasse plaisir à propos du cirque : 'Votre spectacle nous donne du courage.' »
(The only compliment I really appreciate about the circus : 'your show gives us courage.')
Alexandre Bouglione, Cirque Romanès

Draga--*Beloved,*

When I looked into your eyes that first time, I saw the New World there, and I wanted it for my own.

This sentence have I written four times before getting it right: cross out, start again, cross out again, and at last I have said it, in your language. Too hard for me—always the dictionary, always the grammar book, so now, I write what comes.

She goes scarlet-hot all over, Adrian, when she reads that. Stuff it in your pocket, Adrian. Someone might see you with it. One of the other nurses? The intern on duty? Not Hal, at least. It won't burn a hole. Just push it down, down to the tip of the denim triangle, there, flush with your thigh. They don't know anything. It wouldn't be the first time you've had a letter at the hospital. You can read it to your heart's content.

Later.

My Adriana, I want that you know. This is what my house looked like, the one in Srebrenica the Chetniks burned: a big room for cooking and eating, playing cards, playing music, and two for sleeping, children's sleep and parents' sleep. It was sometimes noisy, the parents' room. At nine or ten years old, we figured why. Then we listened extra hard and nudged one another. Wardrobe made of oak, big as a Mafia bodyguard. One round table, six chairs, all the walls hung with rugs my grandmother wove: mostly red, poppy red, sweet-wine red, not blood red. In those days, who thought of blood?

In your house, Adrian, the rugs are on the floor. There's the oval one Grandma hooked, settler style, with remnants from all the dresses she ever made for herself. Yellow, beige, brown, navy blue, pale blue. Plenty.

Adrian pulls off her crepe-soled shoes and walks in thongs to the park, the walled-in one behind the museum, where they broadcast Mozart in the summer from twelve to one. The sun, near its zenith, darts fiery spikes. Adrian slides nearer the stone wall, into the shade. She opens her paper bag, even though she's not hungry.

"You a curator here?" an old woman asked her once, leaning sideways from another bench, when Adrian was unwrapping her ham and cheese. She'd just said no and looked away. Your life story. People are vultures. They always want your life story.

The letter rests in her pocket, hidden treasure, hidden indictment. Today, the garden is deserted. When her fingertips touch the material of her jeans, the paper crackles lightly. Draw it out, before it eats your soul.

One of the darkest hours was when they shot fifty-nine young men on the playing field. The wailing spirits entered into me then and have not left. Me, they did not kill. A Rom is trash anyway to the Gadje, *his death not even worth the trouble. We are black, they say, like dirt on the chimney sweep. Brush us away. Our roof was flimsy and went up in flames easy when the bombs fell right and left, the ones they called the "sows"—fat and ugly and devastating. I will not tell of this, Adriana mine, because it will be too hard for you. I will just say that on that day, I chose life. I did not know it then, but I chose you, for you are my life.*

It's a ploy for sympathy, Adrian; be careful. Who knows if he's making it up? Scarcely a man or boy was left alive in Srebrenica after July eleventh of 1995. She's looked it up in the library. She's read a whole book on it. The thing is, that time he came to the hospital, the scars were there. Wounds tell wicked truths. She doesn't want him to have gone through that. The Dutch troops that failed them, the UN forces deprived of their manhood. Blame who's to blame, Adrian. No Dutchman wanted to harm the Bosnian Muslims of Srebrenica. Nor the Gypsies.

In July of '95, she was already with Hal. Adrian shuts her eyes. In July, they were sailing on Nantucket Sound, while houses burned. While women screamed. While children died. Not her fault, not their fault, not even the fault of the hapless Dutchmen sent to guard.

If only he hadn't been to Oakview Memorial. She could have gone on without knowing all this. When you know things, you become reckless. Live for the moment, he says, for it's the only sure thing. Make love, Adrian, as if your life depends on it. Possibly it does. You know that's what he wants, with his singing blue gaze and soothing gestures. Blue is the true color of Gypsy eyes, he's told her. Is that a story too?

Adriana, you are what's good in this world. You tend, you heal. The Roma, they travel, and I farther than many. I have come to find in your arms my Statue of Liberty, my Declaration of Independence, my own caravan, my voyage home.

Adrian doesn't crumple the letter. She doesn't tear it in a million pieces as she knows she should. At the bottom, below the signature—*Ahmo, with love--*, she has read a place and a time (a street in Brooklyn, three p.m., Saturday). For now, she must go back to work.

༄

O, say, can you see,

Each note is in place except the last-- *"see"*--which leaps onto the tangent of a variation.

By the dawn's early light…

A coy slide into the minor key on *"early light"* draws a titter from the audience, and the national anthem unfurls in a fireworks of exuberant improvisation, as accordion, trombone, and percussion crash joyously into the lone violin's territory. The Gypsy band vibrates with tongue-in-cheek patriotism, as the show takes off:

What so proudly we hailed, at the twilight's last gleaming?

How do they do it? Adrian has heard of resilience, and this is it. Face chaos with a song, the abyss with derision. Spend your last nickel of fortitude on thumbing your nose at fate.

Soon, in full center of the ring, a ripely pregnant young woman begins tossing and catching tenpins in the air in a never-ending arc. She looks composed, amused, surfeited. A pink-and-white gingham dress hugs the ellipse of her belly; dance tights swathe her muscular legs as far as the ankles, discreet, ensuring modesty.

At Adrian's side, Ahmo of the azure eyes watches the performance of Cabaret Cavado ("*Bohemian Family Circus*"). These are his cousins ("*brrotherrs*," he says) from the former Yugoslavia, Tito's, the "democratically" Communist dictator, who let the Gypsies go to school. Here they are performing age-old tricks beneath a red and gold big top pitched among high-rises and shut-down factories. Here stands their Biblical encampment pinched between towering brick bookends.. Ragweed motes and acrid emanations of petroleum pollution surround them on the outside, where fractured, treacherous sidewalk slabs and chain-link fences delimit public and private space.

Inside, in semi-darkness, fresh straw and sawdust bake in honeyed waves of afternoon heat. The Romany circus has squatted (isn't this their custom?) a mangy lot in Brooklyn, and so far the police have turned a blind eye, while neighborhood children and adults alike flock to the celebration.

Ahmo owes these aerialists and fire-eaters his passage across the ocean, his tourist visa, expired now. It's time to go back, Ahmo, but back to where? Tito's Yugoslavia is no more. Back to what? Unhealthier vacant lots than this, where Balkan Gypsies hover before makeshift cabins of mud and planks, hang their tattered laundry only yards away from excrement mounds.

Hal has promised he'll fix her washing machine. If he can't, he'll call someone. He doesn't want her to overdo it. He'll wash her things by hand in the meantime. Anything to make her comfortable. Her days in Emregency are hard enough as it is. Adrian closes her eyes for a moment, and Ajax cans swirl in the place of the calm juggler's wooden pins. She wishes Hal weren't helpful, weren't solicitous, weren't so irreproachably competent and unremittingly possessive.

In the tiers, Ahmo winks at her. But she knows what she knows. He has nowhere to go.

Waiting for a ticket to nowhere doesn't keep him from tapping his foot to the music. He checks to see if she's enjoying herself, raises a dark-brown eyebrow.

Now, there's a hush under the tent, as a diminutive trapeze artist makes her entrance, folded in on herself, borne lightly on the shoulders of a tall, slick-haired man with a red bandanna around his neck. It's part of the Gypsy panoply, Adrian. In front of the footlights, they play themselves, and we eat it up, before we kick them out for trespassing on our lives.

The man stops in front of a heavy rope and lets the young woman grab its rough thickness, then hoist herself from his sturdy torso like the goddess rising from Jupiter's thigh. She climbs to a vertiginous point beneath the tent peak and mounts with graceful, studied application a suspended bar. Adrian sits taut and mesmerized by the girl's intense concentration, the precision and virtuosity of every movement, her entire body a violinist's hand, striking each note right. Unless…

There is no safety net (have the Roma ever lived with safety nets?).

"It's okay, don' worry," interrupts the stout, swarthy ringmaster, his foreign voice gentle, fatherly. "She's got this totally mastered."

That he should so respond to the audience's unspoken anxiety brings a sudden rush of warmth to Adrian's cheeks, a tightening to her throat

As blue as Nantucket Sound on a July day are the eyes of Ahmo the Gyspy who survived Srebrenica. He too has told Adrian not to worry. Reject and burn and even try to exterminate us, and still we tell you, It'll be all right, don't bother your heads. Just admire and applaud us, and we will come back time and again to show you how life is brief but festive and has to be lived right now or never.

My own caravan, my voyage home.

His chestnut hair is damp with sweat, his skin so moist, it clings to hers and makes a suction-cup sound when their thighs come apart.

"Ha! How romantic!" He laughs happily.

Adrian sees yellowed, flowery-cheap wallpaper behind him, a shabby hotel room at five in the afternoon. The summer sun was waxing less lethal *a las cinco de la tarde* (she suddenly remembers this verse), when the toreador died. Not death but life; that's what Ahmo's asking for. You can't give him back the ones the Chetniks took, Adrian; you weren't there. The sailboat on the Sound while Srebrenica agonized—it wasn't your fault, so why do you have to make it up to him? We're not all bad, Ahmo, not all of us.

Just so he understands this. That's all you really want.

MARIAM'S WEDDING GIFT

In three months, September, Mariam's older sister, Haliyeh, will be married to a man she hardly knows, sixteen years her senior, a widower with two children nearly Mariam's age. Haliyeh, at this very moment, is leaning against the darkened windowpane of the room she still shares with her little sister. She looks pensive, as if the dust motes in the shaft of light entering the bedroom had some existential meaning she has to ponder. Her jeans and tee shirt lie piled where they fell alongside the black chador, the lot cast off in defense against the Tehranian heat, and Mariam admires her sister's slender, long-limbed body. Haliyeh's cotton underwear shimmers white against the dark honey of her skin, glistening with a delicate film of perspiration. It crosses Mariam's mind that before long it's the man, "the old man," as she thinks of him, who will contemplate her sister like this, then more than contemplate, according to his desires. The thought frightens her a little.

"Haliyeh?" She can hear the hesitation in her own voice.

"Mmm?"

"Aren't you scared?"

"Scared? About Nasser, you mean?"

Mariam nods. Even if her sister is nine years older, they've always shared a wave-length.

"You know, I'm twenty-seven, and I haven't found anyone. This makes Mother so happy. Someone to take care of me. It's been her main obsession since Father died. Nasser's a doctor." She shrugs. "That means a villa right away, household help. The kids don't bother me. Really, they don't. I like them."

Mariam feels a twinge of annoyance. Is Haliyeh pretending not to know what she means or is she, Mariam, really being a silly child? But what difference does it make, eighteen or twenty-seven, if you've never done it before? "I meant sleeping with him."

She doesn't have to play blasé with her sister, does she? They've always spoken frankly. "Sex," she adds grimly.

"Oh, Mariam." Haliyeh turns toward the younger girl, kneels beside her and gently presses her forearm. "I'm not scared of sex. Just…something else." As soon as the words are out, she thinks she shouldn't have spoken them.

"What?" Mariam's black eyes light up with alarm. "There's something you haven't told me? Is there something wrong with him?"

"Heavens, no! At least, not that I know of. It's me." Now that the subject is out in the open, she might as well plunge ahead. Mariam's eighteen, anyway, not a baby. "There's something wrong with *me*."

"With you? What could be wrong with you? You're beautiful. You're intelligent. You're kind. You're a good Muslim."

Haliyeh looks away: embarrassment? reluctance? "But I'm not a virgin." She tries to guess her sister's expression. She's going to have to turn back and face it.

If Haliyeh had slapped her face, Mariam could not have been more stunned. She looks all at sea on the blue-covered bed where she has been sitting, and her wide, ripe-olive gaze flashes fear.

"Not a…?" The word stays stuck. "But what are you going to do? They know those things, don't they? Men. They're bound to find out. You can't get it back, ever. Haliyeh! When? How? You never told me." Her eyes fill, in spite of herself.

Haliyeh pulls her sister to her, strokes the damp black kinks crushed by the scarf the girl has shed. "You were still little when it happened. I couldn't tell you those things then."

"Tell me now."

"When I was in high school. The grocer's son. You wouldn't remember him. I was the one who ran the errands. We did it in the little warehouse behind the shop. When his father was figuring his accounts. He was sure never to go into the back room then." Haliyeh laughs a little, remembers the shiver, the delicious apprehension of it. Without that, it would have been just groping, and physical, and yes, a little repugnant. She hadn't been in love with the grocer's son but with freedom and defiance. Mariam was right, though. The flower she'd rendered up to him wouldn't grow back. And the doctor could make a nasty fuss. A doctor, of all people. Who better to understand anatomy?

"Weren't you afraid you'd have a baby?" Mariam's voice is hushed. Awe is what she feels now for this big sister so wild, so audacious.

Haliyeh smiles. "He told me he'd know how to pull out in the nick, and he did. Smart guy. But I was crazy. A crazy teenager. A little fool, playing with fire. You're absolutely right. It could have been the end of me. It still may be, in fact. Married one day, repudiated the next. Scandal of the neighborhood, shame and dishonor of her family."

"Stop, Haliyeh! How can you say things like that, as if you were reading the telephone book to me?"

"Because it's going to be all right. Because I have a plan. Don't worry about me, Mariam. Really, it's going to be fine."

This, of course, is when their mother, Najmeh, raps at the door. "Prayer, children," she says. "Grandmother is ready, too. She's waiting for us in the living-room." Najmeh is already decked out in her praying garment of white cloth. A wimp hugs her plump cheeks, preventing the least wisp of her graying hair to escape. It ruffles against her chest, and she pulls the voluminous folds of the cotton tent around and over her already covered head. "Your prayer chadors, Daughters. Look at you!"

"Mother, it's stifling," says Haliyeh. "Aren't you just dying?" Mariam wouldn't have dared, but Haliyeh is grown up and a fiancée now, to boot.

"One comes modest and unspotted before the Almighty."

"Oh, Mother, I can't then. I'd almost forgotten--I'm impure. My period started this morning." Mariam doesn't tell her mother that she has been praying anyway, praying in fact in quiet, occasional parentheses since she awoke, but in a little chamber of her mind, darkened like their bedroom, without paraphernalia, without prostration on the Persian carpet. The little room in her mind has long fingers of sieved sunlight like their room at this hour. It is very peaceful, very comforting, and she retreats there at will. If God minded her period, why would he have made women bleed?

"Then I'll pray for the two of us, for prosperity and fertility in your sister's marriage. Each day we must bring this request before God."

Mariam catches Haliyeh's eye, but her big sister looks bored and abstracted, rummaging already for the cumbersome, immaculate wrap, which she will drape over an outdated dress of plaid seersucker. She kisses Mariam briefly on the forehead; it means, *Don't worry, little one.* All Mariam can think is, *No longer intact. She is no longer intact.* She wills God to make a miracle, to sew her sister up again. She is not spoiled, not violated, only unbarred, disclosed, pierced. All around the invisible, infinitesimal aperture stretches the bakhlava-gold beauty of her skin, of her youthful, curving flesh.

Each day on her way home from secretarial school, Mariam passes a vegetable vendor's. Along the sidewalk, baskets of peppers offer their shiny pouches, round or elongated: green, yellow, red. Farther back, potatoes, onions, and purple egg plant rest in the shade. The merchant, ruddy and black-bearded, sits between his cash register and a pair of tinny scales with a set of weights in a small pyramid by their side. Mariam's gaze usually sweeps over the peppers, sometimes carries as far as the wine-robed egg plant. Today, coincidence has it that she looks up, and a small, white placard in a window above the shop catches her eye. "NIRVANA JEWELRY SALON," she reads. Odd that she has never noticed it before. What could they sell there? She has seen the jewelers in the bazaar with their ample exhibits of gold and silver trinkets. How to attract customers if you don't show your wares? This place must be for insiders, and perhaps it is no question of jewelry at all. With a frisson, Mariam thinks of opium, cocaine, powdery white ecstasies that would land a person in prison. But then, there would be no sign at all. People in the know would just know. She refrains an impulse to ask the vegetable merchant. Tomorrow--she'll ask him tomorrow. She'll buy a pound of something and feign just having seen the sign. A girl can be curious. They may have proclaimed curiosity improper or unbecoming, but to her knowledge, it isn't a full-fledged sin yet. With luck and a little more attention, she may see a customer coming or going. Size them up. And then, who knows, maybe she won't want to find out after all.

Haliyeh and Nasser have been at the family planning center. The course is a prerequisite for a marriage license, and, even though Nasser, as a doctor, could have won exemption, he has wanted his future bride to attend the lectures. A little farther down the street is the "No Scalpel Vasectomy Clinic," but Nasser tells Haliyeh with pride and tenderness that he intends for her to increase the number of his offspring. It doesn't occur to him to ask her opinion. Haliyeh makes a mental note of this but decides not to hold it against him, at least not for the time being. She will have her mental list, yes, ready just in case. You reproach me with this? Then I reproach *you* with this, this, and this.

As they walk sedately side by side (each keeping his hands to himself, naturally), she remembers Mariam's expression when she told her her wedding-night plan. Operation Pseudo-Virginity, she called it, but her younger sister didn't laugh. "You gather nettles from the vacant lot beyond the marketplace (don't forget your gloves). Wash the little crop you've picked. Then sneak the mortar and pestle out of the kitchen. Crush the serrated leaves with the pestle to a dark green paste. Apply internally two hours before bedtime."

Mariam had been horror-sticken. There? Put nettles *there*? You know what they do, just to your arms, your ankles! You'll be all burning, and swollen, and…"

"And, yes! Harder to penetrate than the purest maiden on earth!"

"But Haliyeh, the pain! And what if you're injured for life?"

"Don't be silly! It'll go away. He'll have his wedding night's worth."

"And what about the blood? You're supposed to bleed the first time."

"Nonsense. There's a high percentage of virgins who never bleed. I didn't, in fact. And Nasser's a doctor, so that's not going to be news to him."

"You're sure?"

"Sure, I'm sure. And if he wants blood, there's always a brooch or a sewing needle and a fingertip, after all. But he won't."

"Where, where did you learn this trick?"

"It seems like I've always known it. It's one of the things girls talk about. Some girls, I mean."

"If girls talk about it, then doctors, too, maybe?"

"I'll have to risk it. Maybe, even if he's suspicious, he won't really want to know. I can't see myself in for a medical examination on my wedding night. Come, dear Bride, lie on your back, push up your knees, open wide, that's it, move your bottom closer…"

"You never know! You hardly know him."

"I like him, or I wouldn't have consented to this," she'd told Mariam.

There is something about Nasser's face that pleases Haliyeh. She looks at him now out of the corner of her eye, attracted by the lines on either side of his mouth. They make him look tense, virile, and a trifle unhappy. Haliyeh had heard how he'd mourned his first wife, and this satisfied her. In fact, this, and the lines, had swayed her decision. Nasser had petitioned for her hand for nearly half a year, but she'd asked her mother to let her think about it longer. He'd been kind and persevering, and one day she'd given in.

Mariam makes bold. She is holding two large yellow onions and pretends to glance casually toward the door beside the greengrocer's open-fronted display, as she walks toward the cash register. "Is that the entrance to the jewelry shop over there?" she asks innocently.

The merchant gives her a quick, amused look. "Go see for yourself, Miss. Funny jewelry, if you ask me, but yes, that's the way in."

Relieved, Mariam stuffs the onions into her school bag. She has received neither a lecture nor an admonition. She has got to try it now, or she never will. She pushes open the unlocked door and finds herself in front of a narrow staircase. The stairs are steep; it's the beating of her heart that makes her breathless, along with the weight of her school things. A handwritten sign on a door on the first-floor landing repeats: "Nirvana Jewelry Salon." In smaller letters, awkwardly scrawled, she reads: "Ring bell and please to come in." If it had been a white slavery trap, the vegetable merchant would have told her so, assuredly. He'd have noticed that girls went in and never came out. Assuredly. She is ridiculous to be nervous. Her sister did a lot more than this behind a grocer's. She just wants to see…what they have for sale. She wants to get Haliyeh a wedding gift. Yes! Something pretty to wear. And she hasn't got much money saved. She can't afford the bazaar. She presses on the bell, then on the doorknob. The door gives, and Mariam pushes it open.

A tall young man, black as the ashes from burnt paper, rises from the desk behind which he was sitting. He has on a beige linen tunic with very fine violet stripes. "Hello, welcome, don't be shy" he says, in funny, limping Farsi.

Mariam has rarely seen Africans. The young man's cheeks have a near-reddish sheen in the afternoon light, and she thinks foolishly of cooking chocolate. "I…I came to see," she stammers. "I mean, it says 'Jewelry' on your sign."

"It's a piercing parlor," the boy smiles. "You didn't know? I do noses, mostly. Navels and eyebrows and anything else people ask for, but it's usually noses here in Tehran. I don't have to tell you that girls don't want to uncover themselves." He grins broadly, and suddenly Mariam feels it's going to be all right. She relaxes the grip on her bag. A Bollywood actress with heavily made-up eyes and a strip of glittery stones across her forehead stares at her from a large poster behind the desk. Mariam rapidly takes in a gray, plywood screen in one corner and a table with a set of small instruments beside it. There are bottles, too, and a package of plastic gloves. Close to the window, there is a reclining, black armchair that reminds her of the dentist's.

"Well, no, I didn't know. Piercing? You mean, like Indian women have? That's so beautiful. I never imagined. I was thinking…of a wedding present for my sister."

"Well, then you'd have to send her around."

"You're not from here?" Mariam asks, knowing he isn't.

"Kinshasa. République Démocratique du Congo. Ex-Zaïre. Ex-Belgian Congo," says the boy.

Mariam thinks he might be in his early twenties.

"From so far? All the way from the Congo to a shop in Tehran? "

The boy's smile flashes white again. "I've been places. Learned things. This is a good place to do business. Not much competition. You want to see the studs?"

"Studs?"

"The jewels. For your sister's nose. Or yours, maybe." From the desk drawer, the Congolese boy draws forth a navy-blue velvet-covered plaque. Tiny studs are planted in it like constellations in the night sky. Some are larger than others, some sparkly, others yellow gold or what Mariam takes for silver. "These are white gold," the boy tells her. When they catch the light, they're as bright as diamonds."

Mariam feels a rush of desire; is it what they call covetousness? She wants one of these minuscule stars planted in her nose, in the little dimple just where the swell of the nostril subsides. Instinctively, she touches the spot with her forefinger.

"That's right. It would be nice on you."

"Oh, but I can't."

"Why not? I make special terms. You can pay me in three-four times. The really tiny ones aren't so expensive anyway."

"That's not the only thing." Mariam wants to change the subject. She doesn't want to leave, but she can't tell this boy she will buy his merchandise. "What's your name?" she asks on an impulse.

"Jeremiah."

"A Jewish name?"

"It's in the Bible. That's our Koran, you know. I'm a Christian. My father was more of an animist than anything else, but my mother, she taught the catechism. She brought me up Catholic."

"I thought Africans were Muslims."

"Some are, some aren't. The Belgians brought us their religion, and they're not Muslims."

"And you're allowed to…to make holes in people's bodies like that, in the Catholic religion?"

"Why not? The body's just an envelope. It won't hurt your soul."

Mariam has the impression he's laughing at her. That wouldn't be good business, though, and he has to deal with girls like her here in Iran. Boys, too, maybe. She studies his face with its full mouth, broad, sculpted cheekbones, and high forehead. She hadn't known Africans could be handsome.

"In Africa, there's lots of piercing," Jeremiah goes on. "Traditional. But I learned to do this from a Hindu guy. We were together at a refugee center. I don't know where he's got to, now. I hope he has his jewelry studio too. Somewhere in the world."

Mariam knows she should leave. It would be rude to let him think she's going to be a customer. But she can't bring herself to turn and go. "My name's Mariam," she says. I was just passing by, and I was curious. How did you learn our language?" Asking questions is rude, too, but she thinks the regular rules may not apply with African Catholics. Before Jeremiah can answer her question, a cell phone lying on the desk begins to tootle a four-note jingle. Jeremiah frowns but turns to pick it up. She hears him reply in foreign sounds. When his voice dips into the deeper notes, there is something velvet-whispery about it. She thinks of ashes again, raked smooth. But he sounds annoyed. Mariam must go. Heading abruptly for the door, she makes a sign to him with her free hand.

For a second, Jeremiah presses the phone to his chest. "Come back, Mariam, come another day!" She nods "yes" in spite of herself.

Now, when Mariam approaches the Nirvana Jewelry Salon, she whisks past the vegetable vendor's with a closed, preoccupied look on her face, pushes open the lateral, wooden door and bounds up the stairs. She never spends more than fifteen minutes with Jeremiah—her mother's watch is a precise thing—but from fifteen-minute conversation to fifteen-minute conversation, she has touched a far corner of Jeremiah's world, one so different from hers, she sometimes feels dizzy on her way home. The language he was speaking on the phone that first day, he told her, is called Lingala. His native language, although he'd learned to speak French at school and Farsi since he's been in Iran, four years now.

Lingala, lalala: the name is a song to Mariam. She chanted the syllables all the way back to her room the day she'd learned that, and she hadn't told Haliyeh. Haliyeh has been absorbed with choosing a wedding gown, anyway, and she doesn't need to know the special sing-song that Mariam has stored away in her private, sunlit mental chamber. She likes to think that God speaks Lingala. He speaks every language on all of the earth, and even if you pray with grammar mistakes, he doesn't care. He listens just the same. He doesn't hand out grades for sentence structure. She thinks God doesn't hand out nearly as many grades as people suppose.

Haliyeh's wedding gown, at present laid out on Mariam's blue bed, is a shiny white concoction, as fancy as the iced cake she'll have. It has bulges, and tiers, and peaks of satin down the length of the sleeves and the sides of the long skirt. Nasser will be the only man to see her in it. The women will have their fete apart, where she can parade and show it off. Mariam knows Haliyeh prefers sleek, modern clothes; tight pants and sheathlike sundresses. "How can you stand the prissy, princess stuff?" she asks Haliyeh.

"Your husband's just for you, but your wedding's for everyone," Haliyeh replies. "Mother and Grandmother both clapped when they saw the dress, so I agreed. Why hurt your mother's feelings, when it's only for a day?" If she'd been married at Mariam's age, she'd have protested and sulked, but now, she'll wear a grain sack if it makes them happy. And she'll be a virgin again, as snowy as the gown. Haliyeh represses an ironic smile and strokes the soft, lustrous material.

Mariam has been designated Harvester of Fresh Nettles. Haliyeh won't have time, and her every step before the festivities will be monitored. Mariam can always slip out and back unnoticed. For her sister, she would do not only this but much more, if she could. Mariam feels the need to show Haliyeh how much she loves and admires her. For herself, she fears nothing, but how she hopes there is no risk to Haliyeh's health in this prickly subterfuge! At most, she'll be wretched for the night, Haliyeh has told her. The tissues are sensitive; she'll go easy, she promises. And, yes, she'll make sure no traces of the paste are left. "If Nasser were to get some on himself," she laughs, "he'd wonder at his own swelling!"

"Teach me some words in Lingala," Mariam asks Jeremiah.

"Ah, Lingala, the language of the outstretched hand," he says. "Why?"

"Always my brothers are calling me. Send us money, we have nothing. They imagine, because I sell gold studs and live in the land of petroleum, that I am lolling in wealth. It's true, sometimes I have chicken with my rice. For a chicken leg, a man will kill another in my country."

"How many brothers do you have?"

"One from my mother, five from my father's other wife."

"Catholic men can have more than one wife?"

"My father married his two wives before he converted. The first one, she was always bitching, so he took my mother, too. I would quit answering the telephone, but I'm worried for my mother."

"Why is that?"

"She's in the hospital. Send medecine, they say, too, but I can't do that. Where can I get medicine for what's wrong with my mother?"

Mariam thinks of Nasser. He's a doctor, after all…"What is wrong with your mother?"

"Cancer of the blood."

"Oh, no." Mariam looks at Jeremiah, but he is calm. The adorned Indian movie star on the wall behind his desk suddenly seems incongruous and insolent. "Do you write letters to your mother?"

"In my family we don't write. When you meet up with people, you tell them your news, but letters, we're not used to."

Mariam thinks she may know why. "Can she read?"

"The Bible. A little. My mother, she is like the farmer who builds a wall around his well, every day he carries rocks, even too heavy rocks."

Mariam waits, but the parable seems to be finished. She has noticed how Jeremiah illustrates his thoughts with little stories. Sometimes she guesses at the meaning, sometimes not, but she never interrupts with questions, or Jeremiah will offer another parable to explain the first, and she'll only be more lost. She listens to the Persian words roll off his tongue, and yet she cannot understand half of what he tells her. Every word is correct, even if sometimes the sentences aren't put together quite right. Every word, she could find in the dictionary. Yet all together, they add up to something she cannot follow. Mariam imagines a vast, rock-filled foreign field behind each word that Jeremiah uses. Each one is a signpost for some reality she has never experienced and cannot conjure. Always, she had thought that if you spoke the same language as someone, then you would understand them. Now she knows that mere words are not enough.

Mariam's mother has wanted her to stay home from class this afternoon to help with the tea. Nasser's children are coming with their two grandmothers. She, Najmeh, will be a step-grandmother soon, a member of their ranks, and making the right impression is imperative. Najmeh can get upset over the imperfect ironing of a tablecloth. Each small challenge life places before her she faces like an exam paper. Mariam and Haliyeh bustle in the kitchen, following orders. The confection they are preparing is thick with semolina, drenched in a syrup of clover honey and orange-blossom water. Mariam, who has been grinding walnuts for it, dusts her hands on her apron and cuts a rectangle of aluminum foil from the roll in the pastry drawer. Once the cake has cooled enough to be divided in squares, she'll place one of these in the silvery wrapping and spirit it away under her bed, for Jeremiah to taste. The food in Iran, he has told Mariam, is wonderful, all except the sickening white-sauce the Turk on the corner puts with the kebabs he sells. Jeremiah had tried that, unsuspecting, and hadn't eaten again for twenty-four hours. What an idea, to coat one's food in liquefied wallpaper paste! Mariam guesses there are no sauces in African cooking.

Nasser's children's hands are sticky from the cakes. The little girl, twelve, sits solemnly by her ten-year-old brother. They are on their best behavior, but the sweets have been irresistible. They look curiously at Haliyeh, then at Mariam, until one grandmother tells them not to stare. The girl lowers her eyes obediently, but Haliyeh kneels by her and lifts her chin. "Look at me all you want," she says. "And I'll look at you. You can't be friends with someone you've never seen, can you?" Then she bounds up to retrieve a long-unused pachisi board from the closet. "My sister and I used to play with this. Won't you come along to the garden? We can make a foursome!" The children follow gratefully, as the watchful ladies arrange their features in indulgent half-frowns.

Today, Jeremiah opens the door to his "salon" before Mariam has pressed the bell. "Waiting for you," he says simply.

"Has something happened?" The cake is instantly forgotten. Mariam notices his eyes, black and profound as the well in his story, and too bright today.

"My brother called. Our mother passed away."

Mariam feels tears rise to her own eyes. "I'm sorry. Jeremiah, I'm sorry. Are you going to Kinshasa?"

"Can't go. In spite of what they think, I don't have any money."

She has an idea. "We can pray together. Let's pray. Would you like to? I don't know any Catholic prayers, but you could teach me."

Jeremiah doesn't need to be pressed. He holds out his hands, palms upward, and intones a chant she cannot understand. "That was Lingala," he says softly. "The prayer my mother always taught the children in her Bible class. Now, in French: *Notre père, Qui êtes au Cieux…*" The words and the melody sound different, but Jeremiah's voice is the same, grave and muted. Mariam doesn't think she could repeat any of it.

"I know a beautiful prayer in Arabic," she says. Mariam closes her eyes and recites. When she opens them, she sees thin, parallel streams on Jeremiah's dark cheeks.

"She heard that, my mother did. And God, too," he adds. "Please come another time. I want to give you something in honor of your sister's marriage."

Nasser wrote a very proper message to Najmeh after the tea-party. His children were so cheerful that evening, the letter says. He hadn't seen Laleh like that in months, playful and demonstrative. "Thank you for the wonderful present you are giving me," he goes on to say. That means Haliyeh, naturally.

"He's a romantic, dear, and the children are very well behaved," Najmeh tells her daughter, quite tickled. "But you aren't the only lucky one. I quite agree with what he says!"

A few yards from the greengrocer's, Mariam notices two girls slip through the door to Nirvana, as she thinks of it. She hasn't run into other customers of Jeremiah's, yet she knows he has some. Girls from liberal-minded families, or with eccentric husbands, or maybe, as her mother would surely say, "floozies." Girls who don't care about their reputations and perhaps have none to protect any more. One of the two has a vivid red bolero over her black manteau. A peroxide lock of hair sneaks past the scarf on the second girl's head. Mariam cannot tell which of the two has a nose stud (perhaps both? Perhaps elsewhere on their bodies?)--they have already run off. She climbs the steps to Jeremiah's workshop.

He is beaming this time. "The wedding is soon, right?" he asks Mariam. She nods. "Make your choice." He holds the velvet plaque before Mariam's eyes. "Don't take this kind—they're only cut glass—I want you to have real gold. Yellow or white, which? The only problem is that you may be prettier than the bride."

"Jeremiah, my mother would kill me."

"She'll be too busy to pay attention. If you like it, it's yours."

A thought occurs to Mariam. Of course, she could never detract from Haliyeh's beauty. The idea is absurd. But a piercing…she would share her sister's pain, utterly.

"I'll do it," she says, surprising herself. "Thank you, Jeremiah. Does it hurt?"

"Only for a second. It's over right away. I take all the precautions. Antiseptic, sterilized tool, gloves—you don't have to worry. Just do what I tell you afterward for it to heal up right."

"Only for a second? " she repeats.

"You look disappointed. You want it to hurt?"

"Well, yes, a little, after all. Otherwise, I'm not proving anything."

"You're a funny girl, Mariam."

"I'm tired of being a virgin."

Mariam imagines every reaction her mother might have. She will either faint or scream, she decides. Or else she will tear into Mariam with a scolding such as she's never had before. She tries to steel her nerves for this. It will be like a storm—bound to be over sooner or later, all the more as Mariam will explain coolly to her mother that it isn't irreversible. Later, she'll be able to insert or remove the nose stud as she wishes.

Consequently, Mariam isn't ready for what really happens: torrential, unabated sobbing. And the praying, oh, the praying. The prayer chador is snatched from its shelf, but Mother shuts herself in her room and prays in such a loud voice that only Grandmother, who won't wear her hearing-aid, cannot hear her lamentations. "My little daughter, for shame, for shame! Save her, O, all-wise, all-beneficent One. Only You can see what a trial she is to her poor mother."

Mariam's worry is that Haliyeh will resent the attention drawn away from herself so close to her wedding day, but the elder girl shakes her head in amusement. "You chose the right moment, if you were going to do it," she says. "Mother won't have time to keep this up for too long. As for Grandmother, you're lucky she can't see too well. She may be wanting to squash that pimple on your nose, though."

They dissolve in laughter, as Mariam dunks her nose in a bowl of warm salt-water. Giggling makes her snort, and the water splashes onto their bedroom floor. "If it should get infected, Heaven forbid, at least there'll be a doctor brother-in-law to take care of the wayward teenage sister," Mariam says.

Haliyeh, looking like an ice-cream sundae in her wedding finery, basks good-naturedly in her guests' enthusiasm. To placate her mother, Mariam has drawn her paisley chiffon scarf partly over her right cheek; if it doesn't cover the object of her disgrace, at least the material casts a shadow that makes it harder to pinpoint. In five minutes, it will be time to go for the nettles. She'll have to run past the Nirvana Jewelry Salon on her way to the dusty weed patch where they grow. Before leaving the house, and despite the September sun, Mariam wraps a black chador over her party clothes. She thinks she has been nearly as brave as Haliyeh, even if her own iconic deflowering threatens consequences of lesser gravity. She catches up the folds of her mantle, so that they cover the lower part of her face—this is no time to be stopped in the street by whatever guardians of morality may be lingering there, with nothing better to do than decide what is right for others and what is not. All Mariam knows is that Haliyeh, punctured or repaired, is beautiful and good, and that God loves her. She knows also that Jeremiah is beautiful and good, and that his God—the same one, no?—loves him. And she knows that the precious spangle embedded in the tender "v" at the fore of her right nostril is very beautiful, and that God is smiling at the sight of it.

Morning Sickness

The knife slipped sideways as she sliced off the waxy, red apple peel. Before she knew it, the blade had entered the hollow at the base of her left thumb, paring away more skin: her own, pinkish-white, spouting a sudden, scarlet jet.

« Aïe! » A sharp little yelp escaped her.

His gaze was fixed on the view beyond the kitchen window. Sparrows vied on the backyard lawn for breadcrumbs. She didn't notice his shoulders contract when she cried out. He didn't turn. The light from the window haloed the outline of his dark hair as in a snapshot negative.

« Darn, I've done my finger in, » she said, watching his silhouette. Drops of her blood soaked into a white wedge of apple, turning it rust-colored. She tossed it aside and went to rinse her hand under the cool water of the tap.

« Looks like blood pudding rather than apple pie tonight, » she quipped.

He shrugged imperceptibly and left the room.

Corinne sat with an immaculately bandaged thumb in the third row. « Who's playing Orlando? » she heard someone ask in the polished Oxford tones she'd become used to here..

« Alan Harrington. Requires formidable energy. Not so easy a role to carry off! »

She wondered if anything were easy for him nowadays. She couldn't quite date the moment when it had started, the withdrawal, the moodiness, the birth of that fragile bubble he moved in now. From it, the outside world had shrunk and become unfocused, inaudible. Corinne, above all, despite her presence in his life, had become invisible to him. If she complained that he did not hear her small appeals for help or recognition, he would counter that she was always calling out for nothing. The girl who cried wolf, he would say. How could he know when it was serious from when she'd merely stubbed her toe?

Corinne thought that a stubbed toe deserved some sympathy. Didn't she run to his, to his colds and headaches and bruises? But he never thanked her, seemed, in fact, to find her ministrations both surprising and superfluous. Did he think he deserved to hurt himself?

Corinne remembered parents who'd hugged her and held her on comforting laps when she'd skinned her knees, bumped her elbow, fallen off her bicycle. She remembered kisses for scraped shins. Alan had known Spartan austerity, puritanical rigor, and self-deprivation. His mother had contained her natural outbursts of affection, lest a narcissistic father become jealous and sulk.

She watched Alan stride forward, commanding, charismatic--for his audience, for the ladies Rosalind and Celia, stage right, both so worried about the young gentleman's fate.

Captivated, Corinne watched him cheer Rosalind and, finally, victorious in the wrestling match, win her heart. She saw an Alan she'd forgotten: intense, tender, playful. His elegant accent thrilled her, when earlier it had risen like a wrought-iron gate between them. She rejoiced at Orlando's wedding to Rosalind, and her heart rose on a crest of hope when the actress admonished, in her epilogue:

(...) and I charge you, O men! for the love you bear to women (...) that between you and the women, the play may please.

Alan took innumerable curtain calls, bowing with unfeigned pleasure and the actor's elegant good breeding. He radiated competence and benevolence. Corinne's eyes misted over. She was proud of him, so proud. And she would be Rosalind to him, now. She would be the one enfolded in his arms, reassured and wooed and cherished.

Alan's director shifted his champagne glass and pressed Corinne's hand. « So,what do you think of our *As You Like It*?" He noticed the tight, white « dolly » her left thumb made. "Ah, but what have you done to yourself, Mrs. Harrington? »

« A little kitchen mishap. Nothing at all, » she said, laughing it off, listening to herself, careful to keep the twang out of her voice. « And the play was wonderful. I am dizzy with admiration. However did you teach Alan to wrestle like that? »

As if on cue, Alan moved beside her, sliding his arm through hers. « The fact is, I've been hiding my new athletic prowess from my wife. I wanted her to be surprised. » He drew Corinne closer to his side, his head tilted ever so slightly toward hers, pleased with her or pleased with himself? He had every right to the latter, but she wished so fervently he might be proud of her, too.

She remembered suddenly how, fishing for compliments one day, she'd asked him if he didn't find her younger, more stylish than an acquaintance they'd run into the day before. To her mind, there was no doubt about the matter, but this was how low she'd fallen, how desperate she'd been for one appreciative word from him.

« Have you taken a look at yourself in the mirror recently? » he'd replied coldly. Corinne winced at the recollection. The words had cut more deeply than the paring knife this morning, and the wound would not heal so quickly.

But this evening, inebriated with Shakespeare and success, he showed her off to his fellow actors: « My wife, Corinne, a published poet in the United States and professor of American literature. » She read respect and admiration on their faces. Not a trace of condescension. Did he perceive it too? Yes, it was reflected in his clear, gray eyes as he toured the crowded room with her. When she looked at him, she saw only Orlando, sincere and smitten, and she was sure Alan had touched home.

The telephone woke Corinne from an uneasy sleep. She'd skipped her period, and for five days now, her stomach had churned each morning at dawn. The queasy feeling had dogged her until noon.

« They've added on rehearsals, » Alan told her, returning to their bedroom. « We've got to go over some scenes with Jacques' understudy. I have to be there in forty-five minutes. »

Corinne turned toward him. « Alan, I'm nauseated, » she said carefully, certain she wasn't whining. « It's been going on for some time. You know, like...morning sickness? »

What those words augured; how would he take it?

« Mmm. I'll get the coffee. Want some? »

« I couldn't possibly... »

« OK, see you later, then. » The bedroom door clicked behind him.

Shutting her eyes, she imagined him outlined against the kitchen window, his shoulders steady, his back to her. As she buried her forehead in the pillow, a greenish wave surged and fell in the depths of her.

Blows To The Heart

Annabelle had a perfect, pale oval of a face and blue puppy-dog eyes that flashed helplessness and resignation like twin beacons over a bay. Her first words to Candace were, "*Madame, je suis cardiaque. Je vais bientôt m'absenter pour me faire opérer du coeur.*" A heart operation, and soon. She'd have to miss school.

Candace was appalled. The poor girl's parents. Surely worried sick. Not to mention Annabelle herself. Yet she cultivated a brave, detached air. Candace admired how the girl held herself, head high, her books clutched against her right breast. It was under the left one that something was awry. "What's the problem, exactly?" Candace dared to ask.

"It gets to beating too fast, and then I suffocate," Annabelle answered. "I feel like I'm going to pass out. Please forgive me if I seem half-asleep in class. It's the medicine I have to take."

Candace nodded sympathetically. "Of course. I understand. Don't overextend yourself." She studiously avoided questioning the girl after that. Lessons learned or not learned, what did it matter, really, when every day might be your last? Annabelle's first written paper was a catastrophe. She scrawled English in a gray shade of ball-point that somehow reminded Candace of the girl's indocile hair. The letters turned every which way, and the words were full of misplaced *s*'s; the sentences were broken, nearly incoherent. Candace wracked her brain for something kind to say, some encouragement for the top of the first page. She wrote in fuschia; red ink was too much like blood. "*Foundations a bit weak. You'll need to make progress this year.*"

Annabelle didn't appear unduly perturbed by her weak grade. Candace saw her shrug and whisper something to her neighbor, Elodie. Candace's French high school seniors sat at tables lined in rows of three or four. Between the series of rows was a central aisle, down which she could stroll, looking from side to side, making sure homework had been done, notes were dutifully being taken, exercises completed.

Elodie's notebook showed nothing but sketches. *"Draw Dr. T.J. Eckleburg's eyes as F. Scott Fitzgerald describes them,*" Candace had asked the class. They pored over the second chapter of *Gatsby*, puzzling out the foreign idioms of the description. Elodie had given a pear-shaped nose, a bristly mustache, and a goatee to Fitzgerald's disembodied oculist. She was careful with the details of a stethoscope hanging askew on his chest. When Candace suggested she consult the text again, just to be sure she'd understood, Elodie replied, "I made him the way I wanted to," with an I-dare-you-to-challenge-me pout.

Candace was no newcomer to the subtly smoldering rebelliousness of teenage girls. She assumed American ones were the same as these, more impertinent even, although she'd never taught in an American high school. Her qualifications here were in English and *lettres*, but at home her subject would more likely be recognized as "EFL," English as a Foreign Language. *The Great Gatsby* was on the national syllabus, *le Programme*, and the class would have to bear with it. Candace loved it, adored Gatsby's extravagant bashes, the lavish Long Island manors; she vibrated to distant strains of the Charleston and felt the oppressive heat of that New York summer penetrate her own skin. She understood that her students could neither hear nor feel these things, yet it remained a constant source of frustration that she was in no way able to communicate to them the opulence of Fitzgerald's style, the flowing, rippling tide that buoyed his prose. If you like something, then never teach it to teenagers, she thought to herself, wondering if she'd become a true cynic. Keep it, treasure it, don't expose it to the philistines.

Annabelle didn't even attempt the drawing and admitted frankly that she hadn't understood the second and third questions either: "*Pick out the negative words in the description of the ' valley of ashes.' What does the valley remind you of?"* So, she had skipped them, she said matter-of-factly. Unlike Elodie, she never tried to hide her incompetence behind an air of insolence. Candace thought illness had made her mature. Or was she simply better natured?

On the first day back after midterm break, Candace made a mild effort at joviality. "How are you?" she asked the group hospitably. "Rested up?" Thirty girls swerved their gaze to the side, avoiding eye-contact with her. She didn't take it personally. It wasn't her they disliked, just the whole idea of foreign literature from four to five in the afternoon, an impossible novel they couldn't make out, too many questions, too many obligations. Still, she remembered other late-hour lit classes that had "worked," as her fellow teachers said. The students had vied with one another to have the floor, to hazard a guess, to analyze a character's behavior in the light of their own adolescent experience. This year's crew was unusually subdued, even sullen. Candace felt indefinable discomfort in their presence, even if she couldn't put a finger on the cause. Possibly they were afraid of one another.

Candace spent an inordinate amount of time preparing supper that evening. Slicing, stirring, paring were physical operations that relaxed her. She propped open her French cookbook to *Boeuf Bourguignon.* She chopped the slabs of beef methodically into cubes, then went to the cellar for a bottle of red wine. When the sauce was ready, it had the rich texture of burgundy-shaded velour.

"Didier," she spoke abruptly. "I've had it."

"Had what?" He looked alarmed.

"Oh, gosh, nothing to do with you! Had it with teaching recalcitrant teens."

"Come on, Candie, you've felt this before. Recalcitrant teens are your daily bread. What else can you do?"

Candace knew this was true. If you can't do, teach, and she taught. As much as she hated the scornful adage she assumed it applied in her case. The only things in the world she managed with any competence were speaking foreign languages and analyzing literary texts. Those skills didn't necessarily make for success in everyday life. She had the laurels, the sheepskins. She did what she could, put her heart into it day after day, but she couldn't peddle her merchandise with conviction any more. Annabelle's face came back to her, blandly self-accepting above the conundrum of the pages. *I'm no good, but who cares?* Elodie's defiant smirk said the contrary: *I'd be good, if only you'd give us something worth bothering about.*

Candace sighed. "I'm ready to go home," she said.

"Candace, you *are* home," Didier replied, putting down his fork. "You signed on for a French husband, French citizenship, a French job with a French administration... Are you sure you want to throw it all over?"

"I'll keep you," she relented, smiling, "and the citizenship, since it goes with you. But the job is just too much. The security of it is killing me."

"What do you mean, killing you?"

"Exactly. Everyone dreams of job security, but it's like handcuffs. It hinders movement. You can't take your fate into your own hands any more. There's just too much comfort you'd be losing. So you stay, but your hands are tied."

"*Ma chérie*, you've just had a bad day!"

"No worse than most. That's the thing. Little by little you become tolerant of all the little disappointments, the disinterest, the hostility, even. All the little "*coups au coeur*"—blows to the heart. You start growing a second epidermis like an oilskin, and everything slides off it, but that indifference isn't really you. It's an emotional protection you can't live without after a while. By the way, speaking of "*coeur*," do you know I've got a student this year with some sort of heart trouble?"

"You haven't mentioned it. A girl? A boy?"

"A girl. In the seniors. You know, there're only girls in that class anyway. Only girls would take optional English lit."

"Is she a good student?"

"No, very poor. But she clearly doesn't mind. I guess I wouldn't either, if I had heart disease. Must give you a real sense of perspective. I don't even know if she likes English or if she took the class because she needed an elective. Mainly, I hope I won't do her in altogether with Fitzgerald!"

"I think she might be glad to have you for that course."

"Didier, they only appreciate you when they've had someone worse. A sub. A trainee."

"Come on, don't be hard on yourself. And I'll bet things'll go better tomorrow. You'll enjoy the kids, for one reason or another. Every profession has its ups and downs."

Candace didn't enjoy them any better. In fact, she didn't know what to think. Farida, a dark-haired girl of Moroccan descent, had been absent for three weeks, but today she made a guest appearance. Candace asked her for her signed excuse; according to rule, it had to appear in a pale, blue notebook, called *carnet de correspondance*. Without which, a teacher was not to accept a student in class after an absence.

"I don't have it on me," Farida said simply.

Candace was loth to send the girl away, when she'd already missed so much. Moreover, Farida had a "history." She was an inveterate class-cutter, but everyone also knew she'd made a suicide attempt—an overdose of sleeping pills-- during her first year in high school. "Next time, then, without fail?"

Farida nodded and took her seat. No more than five minutes of class had gone by, when Candace saw her leap up and bound for the door. Ideas ran immediately through Candace's mind: she's got to get to the toilet; she's overdosing, freaking out; she swallowed something she shouldn't have… "Please, someone go after her," she said, and Elodie rose promptly from her seat. They returned twenty minutes later, Farida's complexion faintly yellow. Another student I mustn't question about her work, Candace thought. Who next?

She approached the girl after the hour was up. "What happened to you, Farida?" she said. "Are you all right , now?"

"Not really," the girl replied. "It's the Ramadan. I'm fasting."

"And you felt ill?"

"Yes. I had a sharp pain in my stomach."

"Maybe, if it makes you ill, you could request a dispensation? I mean, if you wanted to, of course."

"Yes, but I don't want one."

Naturally not, thought Candace. It was more interesting to fall dramatically ill in the middle of class and more convenient to have a legitimate excuse to escape regularly to the infirmary.

Candace decided it was time to see the head teacher about the class. *Les jeunes filles en fleur* were falling by the wayside. Elodie was still drawing elaborate pictures thoughout the lessons; Farida was absent again, and Annabelle had said some things Candace found odd. " I think I'll have my operation soon," she'd confided before class. "I've started throwing up blood again." Candace frowned with concern but afterwards pondered the girl's words. Did you "think" you'd have an operation, or did a doctor order one? Was spitting up blood—this, she didn't question, or at least would not, for the time being—a heart symptom? Something else? A digestive problem, wouldn't it be? The girl was a probably a bundle of nerves; her heart trouble could be tachycardia and she could have an ulcer.

Moreover, Candace was putting two and two together and finding "untruth" as the sum. The questionnaire Annabelle had filled out at the beginning of school said that she lived alone in an apartment and worked on weekends. What parents would let their eighteen-year-old daughter, gravely ill, stay alone and leave her to shoulder a job in addition to school? The last year of French high school was no joke: the national examination, *le Bac*, loomed in June and July; the entire country took it seriously. Rare were the *lycée* students who held part-time jobs. Mythomania? wondered Candace. A ploy for sympathy? A well-thought-out justification for her failings at school? A handy excuse for not turning work in? She stopped feeling sorry for Annabelle, although she would never let on her doubts. What if, in spite of it all, the girl's claims were true?

She told Monsieur Mathieu her misgivings. Monsieur Mathieu, the form's head teacher, was the only one of her colleagues she called "*Monsieur*" and said "*vous*" to. *Vous* was courteous and respectful, the formal *you*. This was, of course, because he said *Madame* and *vous* to her. She called her other colleagues by their first names and used the familiar "*tu*" with them. They were all former university students overgrown, and no hierarchy set them apart. But Monsieur Mathieu was of some older school. He wore a felt hat to work and a belted, black overcoat. He expressed himself with refined elegance yet not a trace of pedantry.

"I'll summon each one to a conference," he said. "Presence at school is not optional. One doesn't choose one's classes *à la carte*. As for the young Annabelle, yes, she has spoken to me of her heart condition. What you say sheds a new light on the matter, however. And as far as her friend is concerned..." He pointed to the photograph of Elodie on the class identity sheet.

"This one poses another problem. One can see she's *hypervitaminée.*"

Candace wondered what he could mean by "hypervitamined." Overfed with vitamins? She looked at Elodie's plump, juvenile face, her cropped brown hair stuck in myriad little tails, gluey with the gel young people used.

"This one," Monsieur Mathieu continued, "opened her veins last year." He ran his left forefinger graphically along the inside of his right wrist. "And she suffers from anorexia."

How did he know these things? Candace wondered. Anorexia most certainly was not written on Elodie's round cheeks. No doubt she'd confided all this on some beginning-of-the-year file card. She and Annabelle were accomplices, then, in teenage *mal de vivre.* Did they bolster each other or, on the contrary, lead each other hand in hand down paths of misery and marginality? And I, she thought, obstinately require them to write literary commentary on pages as far removed from their lives as if they were engraved in hieroglyphics.

As always, Candace chose her clothes carefully before school. She had to look young and hip but not too much so. She had to look authoritative but not austere. The navy blue slacks gave her an enviable figure, she knew, and the cut was the latest. She wore a jacket with a tailored look to it; professional and just a bit original. She ought to depend on her own qualities to give her confidence, not on rags, she thought. But clothes were reassuring. For her, they were the costume an actress slips on as she slides into a character. Candace's role in the French high school was *Madame le professeur d'anglais.* It demanded a tight-rope act between severity and a gentle, open-minded readiness to listen. And, indeed, she would listen willingly, on condition the confidences she gathered were trustworthy, not crafty or manipulative. She was no longer sure what to think of Annabelle, Elodie, and Farida. Illness or hypochondria? Religious fervor or a compulsion to show off? Self-hate or social unease? Candace would see her senior literary form at ten.

The girls lined up to the side of Candace's desk, which stood on the *estrade*, the platform. Today, everyone was to hand in an *explication de texte*: written commentary of a passage from *The*

Great Gatsby, in the purest scholarly fashion *à la française.* No sketches or underlining of words this time: the commentary was to prepare them for their national exam. Each in turn offered an excuse for not having done her work. "Madame, I know it sounds crazy, but I didn't have my book with me last night; somehow or other, it got into Anne-Laure's bag…"; "Madame, I was behind on my philosophy paper, and I couldn't, I just couldn't…"; "Would it be all right if I put it in your pigeon-hole this afternoon?"; "Will you still accept it tomorrow?"

"Hand it in when you're ready," Candace replied, jaded. "Good excuses, bad excuses, it's all the same price: one point off per late day." They knew the "fee," but they would try, anyway. She supposed it was human nature. Trying to get away with shirking one's responsibilities. She noticed that neither Annabelle nor Elodie had asked to be let off the hook. Farida was absent.

When the bell had rung and the girls filed out, Candace thumbed through the handwritten papers still piled in a corner on her desk. She found none from Annabelle, none from Elodie. Candace dropped the collection into her dark green leather satchel, shrugged her purse strap over her shoulder, and moved on to another room, where her next class was scheduled.

Candace spent an hour that evening reading several American college catalogues she'd garnered. "I could apply to this one," she told Didier. Their French department has a good reputation, and I have all the qualifications. I don't *have* to spend my life stuffing English down Gallic throats."

He bent over her shoulder, studying the bell tower and the spectacular autumn views of New England foliage. "*Et moi?* What would I do there," he asked. "Offer a course in French *cuisine*?"

"Well, for a start. And then you could open a crèpe restaurant…," Candace teased. She knew it was hopeless. Didier was happy in his work here as a biochemist, and his English was despicable. She was the polyglot, the transplantation artist. It was up to her to make the sacrifice. There would always be summer vacations.

She sighed and turned to her papers. The commentaries were appearing in her pigeon-hole mailbox in small, progressive batches. She was happy that Elodie was only one day late—only one point to take off. Annabelle's scribbling didn't appear until the end of the week, and she handed it in in person.

"If I'm late, you understand why, of course, Madame," she'd said, as though it went without saying that her heart condition—vomiting blood, *n'est-ce pas*?--had kept her from sitting down to her work during the two weeks she'd had to do it in. She'd made a visible effort, brought forth four long pages of half-coherent English in what must have been bitter birth pangs. She turned her back and moved away before Candace could question her further.

She wrote carefully across the top of Annabelle's paper: *If your state of health has prevented you from turning this in on time, then please provide a doctor's certificate or a letter from your parents.* In the meantime, she subtracted the four points: Tuesday, Wednesday, Thursday, Friday. Despite the surface of paper Annabelle had managed to cover in gray ink, she had a failing grade.

"If I bring in the certificate, will you add back the four points?" she asked, as Candace toured her classroom, calling names, distributing papers right and left.

"Well, yes," she replied, "depending on what it says, naturally." Candace noticed her stuff the paper casually into her book bag. She didn't bother to puzzle over the innumerable corrections and asides in the margin. Still, the four points had seemed to interest her. Why have asked that question, if everything, work, grades, success or failure, were utterly indifferent to her?

Candace expected the doctor's note any day, but it never came. Nor did Annabelle's parents write. Had she even bothered to ask them, or was it all a hoax after all? Candace noticed the girl's wan complexion and felt a twinge of compunction for suspecting her. Probably, poor, tired Annabelle was too discouraged to care.

The Christmas holidays approached and the inevitable cases of flu. Annabelle, however, never missed class. She never again mentioned her impending heart surgery, either, but, like Farida, had failed to hand in her last paper entirely. Candace wrote "0" in the column opposite the girl's name in the purple grade book she always carried with her. Annabelle looked pained and longsuffering, as Candace toured the room, handing back corrected copies. Elodie, claiming her grandfather had passed away, had requested an extension. Not wanting to delve further, Candace had granted it. She expected Annabelle to come to her desk after class with some story of suffocation or palpitations and ask for a make-up assignment, but she didn't.

"I should have called her to me" Candace told Didier afterward, as they sat over supper. "I shouldn't have let her leave the room like that, no questions asked."

"But you told me she's eighteen and lives alone, didn't you?" He leaned against his chair back and tucked his chin into his collar.

Candace agreed this was true. Still, she had little appetite that evening for the onion soup she'd made. She twisted the limp, translucent slices around her spoon.

"The kid accepted her zero. She paid the price," he went on. "They have to grow up sooner or later and recognize that their acts have consequences. And she seems to be doing just that. Why insist?"

"Well, because she's just a girl. She's troubled about something."

From the end of the corridor, Candace could see a small group of her students huddled in front of the classroom where they met at ten on Tuesdays. That in itself was unremarkable. They always waited for her to come with her key and open the room for them after the morning break. Today, she thought they looked particularly glum, or was it her imagination? As she rummaged in her bag for the door key, she thought she heard someone say in a flat, low voice, "No one's allowed to visit. Only immediate family."

Candace surveyed the class, once everyone had arrived. Usually she counted the number of students first and could take the roll at a glance, although, with so many young faces to keep track of, she sometimes hesitated. Which one or ones were absent? She hated to bother with the formal roll call and, if the number didn't tally, usually asked, "Well, can someone tell me who's not here today?" If the group wanted to cover up for someone, they would look back at her blankly, hoping ever naively that she wouldn't discover who, would forget to note it down on the special roll sheet . But she would pull out her list and call their names in alphabetical order, not last name first as always in French schools (Dupont Marie, Durand Hélène…), but, more gently, just their first names or first, then last. Annabelle Ricard, she said, realizing suddenly, all the way down into the R's, that it was Annabelle who was missing.

"*Elle est hospitalisée, Madame*," the class leader volunteered. An earnest, hazel-eyed girl with scarlet plastic-rimmed glasses.

"Hospitalized?" Candace was alarmed. "Her heart trouble? *C'est son coeur*?"

The girl shook her head. "We don't know. The hospital's not giving out any information."

Candace felt her throat grip, the way it did sometimes when she was tense. Elodie was quiet, staring at her closed notebook. "Tell me, will you," she asked the class, "when you find out something?"

The leader nodded. "*Oui, Madame.* »

When her teaching hours were over, Candace called the public hospital from her study at home. The hospital was a huge place. What unit was she in, the receptionist wanted to know. Candace hesitated: *Cardiologie*? But in the meantime, the girl had found Ricard Annabelle on her computer screen. "Her condition is stable. No visitors. We're sorry."

Candace kept seeing the zero opposite Annabelle's name in the lined columns of her grade book. She remembered her demand for a medical certificate or a letter from the girl's parents. Perhaps she was in conflict with them, had moved out to get away from an unhealthy atmosphere, some perversity—who knew?—one heard such appalling things these days. And of course she had to have a part-time job in order to pay her own rent. Her heart—whatever the problem was--malformation, disease—had been overstrained by too many demands. Candace felt her own heart skip a beat and flutter irregularly. Extrasystoles. She knew what they felt like. But it was nerves, just nerves.

She knew she wouldn't sleep that night if she couldn't find out more. Candace climbed into her little French car—a squat, white Twingo—and drove through the meanders of the impressive *Centre Hospitalier.* She had never been there before, had had no idea her town contained such a city within the city. The guard at the entrance had indicated a flat-faced, beige stucco building whose left wing, he assured, housed the cardiology division. When at last she had found it, there were no spaces left in the parking-lot in front, and Candace had to drive back toward Maternity, then walk past rows of cars, hurried personnel in uniform, preoccupied-looking visitors bearing all manner of plastic bags, plants, and bouquets.

"Annabelle Ricard?" asked the girl at the desk. "Hmm, Ricard, Ricard...No, she's not here."

"But she must be," Candace insisted. "I know she's hospitalized."

"Maybe in another *service*, then," the receptionist suggested. "Let me just check. Ah, yes, she's in *Psychiatrie. Maladies Nerveuses*," she specified, taking Candace's puzzled look for ignorance of the word. She tapped lightly on the screen. "It says here: *pas de visite.*"

"I know," said Candace. "Thank you. Where is *Psychiatrie*?"

In the downstairs lobby of the psychiatric unit, Candace immediately spotted Elodie and two other girls from the class. "Ah, Madame, you've come for Annabelle?" said one, rising to meet her. She had a nutmeg-dusted complexion and a heavy, blond braid down her back, like a Valkyrie. A slender, steel pin pierced the tip of her left eyebrow.

"Yes, for Annabelle. How is she? What's happened? Why the psychiatric department?"

"It's depression," another replied, rising in turn. She was dressed in an ankle-length, fitted black coat and wore heavy, ink-black eye make-up. The raven out of Poe. Her lips were painted a brownish shade of violet and outlined in black. "She, uh...*elle a fait une bêtise.* » She did something foolish.

Candace knew what that meant. "Oh, no! Will she be all right? Do you know?"

"Yes, we've seen a nurse from her floor."

"And her parents? Aren't her parents here?"

The Valkyrie shrugged. "I'm sure they've come, but we didn't see them. Annabelle's on good terms with her parents, but she moved out to live with her boyfriend."

Not alone, then, Candace thought. "And her boyfriend…?"

"Well, that was the problem," the Addams-cartoon girl replied, rubbing some of her dark coat cloth between thumb and forefinger like a security blanket. She glanced toward Elodie, as if for permission to go on with her story. Elodie merely stared into space.

"He was arrested for dealing shit."

Annabelle's words came back to Candace suddenly: "*Please forgive me if I'm half-asleep…it's the medicine…*" So, was that it? But why this sudden fit of despair? "But it's not because he was arrested, that she…that she…?"

"No," the girl said. "But she was scared of staying alone. She said her parents wouldn't take her back, and with her heart problem—well, they were going to have to graft some sort of device into her…she said she didn't want it, that she'd never live long anyway…" Already *la jeune fille gothique* was turning away, as if she regretted having said too much.

Candace found the explanations contradictory, implausible, and distressing. "If you get to visit, please greet her for me. Tell her to take care of herself, to get well soon."

"*Oui, Madame.*" The group of girls closed in again on itself, excluding Candace and her insistent good will.

Driving home, Candace thought she'd tell Monsieur Mathieu about the situation as soon as possible, perhaps call him that evening. He, in turn, would write up little notes for each teacher of the class and distribute them to their pigeon-holes in the staff room. It was better they be warned than risk a faux pas, expressing suspicion or disapproval or scolding the girl for missing class.

Annabelle was absent only three days. Being of age, she had filled out and signed her *carnet de correspondance* herself: *absente pour raisons de santé,* health reasons. Candace saw that it had been properly stamped by the Office downstairs. Her head high as usual, the girl placed it on Candace's desk before the lesson; her committee of friends stood in the background, vigilant, hovering.

A rose-colored fire seemed to have kindled beneath Annabelle's pale skin, and as the girls moved slowly toward their seats in the last row, Candace had the impression they were bearing their sickly classmate in triumph on invisible shoulders. She picked up whispering among the incoming tide of students: *Much more than Farida…nearly a whole bottle of vodka with the pills…After* my *last attempt…* She thought briefly of Fitzgerald's metaphorical valley of ashes. Wasn't it, after all, a place these child-women inhabited?

Candace carried the large envelope with the application form to the post office. She didn't dare drop it into the rectangular, yellow mailbox fixated to the wall below her apartment building. The postage might be insufficient. Moreover, she wanted to see the employee glue on it the navy blue "*prioritaire*" sticker.

If they were interested in her, there would be plenty of time to tell Didier. Together, they'd figure something out. There was a chemistry department at the college, a highly-reputed one, too. She'd tutor him in English day and night. American college students were a little grown up, after all, or so she thought. They weren't exempt from heartbreak, maybe, but they could still force a smile at life. They'd transcended the throes of revolt. They didn't wear their souls on their lapels. Candace felt sure they did not.

Olive in Two Languages

Olive likes saying her name in English: *AH-Liv.* It's in Henry James, Maman said, and his Olive is a very pretty lady. In French it's nothing but a little, shiny, round fruit: *O-LEEV.* Accent on the second syllable, please. She prefers herself in English: the beautiful lady, *la belle dame.* Besides, when you switch the letters around, they make *I Love.*

« Olive » is also for the Mediterranean, Maman said. For the sea and peace and Greek temples all sparkling in the sun. Daddy's the one who chose her name, before she was born even.

She clings to the memory now of what it was like, when he held her in his arms. She would ride around on his shoulders and smell the clean, white laundry smell of his office shirt. *Son bleu de travail,* he used to joke. His work overalls. Daddy's French was good, but he was English. That's why Olive speaks English.

« *Je parle anglais. Et vous*? Do you speak English, Monsieur? »

« A little, » the man said. It sounded like « a LEEtle, » like the end of her name, the French way. He was sitting on a bench in the park, and beside him was a huge canvas backpack, all out of shape and torn and discolored. He had his arm around it, like a fiancée.

« What's in your bag, Monsieur? » asked Olive.

« Leetle girl curiosity, eh? » asked the man. His complexion was brown and his cheeks a little hollow. Spiky black bristles stood out on his chin and above his upper lip. He smiled at Olive, and the white of his teeth flashed just like one of those sunlit Greek columns. It made her feel warm. Mediterranean sun.

Calais was chilly in November. Maman had made her wear her dove-gray anorak, the one with the fake-fur collar and the pink lining. « Remember, I can see you from the balcony, » she'd said to Olive. « You can walk along the pyracantha, but don't go away from the fence. *C'est promis?* »

« I promise, » Olive had said. Pyracantha; that meant firethorn. She'd gathered up a whole hankyful of bright, orange-red berries from the bushes near the black fence, the wrought-iron grille. If she could find a squirrel, she would try and feed them to it. That was when she'd seen the man. He looked tired and discouraged and very poor.

« In my bag, » he said, answering Olive's question, « are everytheeng I need for Eengland. »

« *Vous allez en Angleterre*? » Olive was so surprised, she lapsed back into French. He didn't look like the tourists that climbed on the ferry. « Is that your suitcase? And your guidebook? Do you have one? »

The man smiled again, his warm sun smile, and said no, he didn't have any need of a guidebook. He knew someone who was going to show him the way. He was going to England to stay, forever. And then to bring his family. His wife, his little girl. A little girl like Olive, but with black hair, not golden.

« Why aren't they with you now? » Olive asked, suddenly distressed. Another daddy, going to England. Maybe, like hers, he would never call for his little girl.

« Treep too deeficult, » he said. « Later, they come. When I get work and money, lots of money to pay for passage. »

« Please, what's her name? *Elle s'appelle comment, votre fille*? »

« Sorayya her name, » he said. « You want see peecture? I show you, Meess. » From the depths of his battered bag, he drew a small plastic square. It was a little greasy-blurry, like Maman's glasses, when she'd accidentally put a finger on the lenses. Through the smudgy plastic, a little girl stared. She had very big, very serious black eyes. A navy blue scarf covered most of her hair, and two ends of it crossed beneath her chin.

« Why does she have a scarf? Is it cold where you're from? »

« Tradeetion. Sometimes cold, sometimes not. In Eengland, she no more wear scarf. Be like Eenglish girls. Wind in hair. Hair fly like blackbird weeng. Here bracelet from her. I keep to think of her. » From an outer pocket of the backpack, he pulled a tarnished, copper-colored circlet.

« Don't you miss her? »

« Very much, I meess. »

« Why didn't you stay with her? » In spite of herself, Olive felt something tight in her throat when she asked this.

« No good for leetle girls in my country. Bad men break everytheeng. In Eengland, everytheeng good. Lots work for poor men. Nice people, don' ask for papers all day long. Cheeldren go to school. Good food to eat. »

« *Olive! Dépêche-toi!* Hurry up! » Maman was calling.

Olive heard her name, *son nom français*. She had to go back. « Is your boat tonight? » she asked the man.

« I don' theenk so. »

« Then where will you go? Will you get your supper? »

The man shook his head. « I sleep here. Nice park, nice bench. But cold in France. Sangatte center shut, they don' let me een. So I wait here. Wait for friend who show me the way. »

« O-LEEV! »

« *Au revoir*, Monsieur. Bye-bye! »

Olive looked both ways and ran to the apartment building across the street.

༄

She had a crusty *baguette* for the backpack man, the kind she liked best, with the inside all soft-white and chewy. She'd saved her chocolate from her four o'clock *goûter*, and Maman would never notice the missing apples. Olive had had an idea last night, before she'd fallen asleep. Let him still be here, she'd thought, as she drifted off. Please let him still be here. Let him not be gone, not yet, *pas encore, pas encore...*

He was there, the deep tan of his face slightly ruddy in the cold afternoon light, the black bristles of his chin a little longer. He smiled his marble-white smile at Olive and took the bread with a «Thank you, leetle mademoiselle. »

« Monsieur, Sir, please, pretty please, *s'il vous plaît*, » she said, « Will you do something for me? »

« What can I do for you? » he asked, his black eyebrows puzzling together.

« When you are in England... »

« Yes...? »

« When you are in England, will you look for my daddy for me and give him a message? »

« Your daddy in Eengland? »

« Yes. »

« Eengland very beeg place. Where I look? London? »

« Yes, London. To begin. Mr. Donald Davenport. And my name is Olive. » She said AH-liv. « Tell him I want him to have me come. Like Sorayya, for you. Please, will you? »

« I don' understand. Your daddy in Eengland; he don' call for you? You don' veezit? »

Olive's eyes filled, and the man stopped his questions.

« You don' cry, » he said, touching her hand. « I look for daddy for you. Write name on piece paper, OK? »

On Wednesday, there was no school in the afternoon, and Olive went earlier to the park, but on the bench were two teenagers from the *lycée*, the high school down the street. As the girl leaned toward the boy to offer her mouth for kissing, her tight, short pullover rode up and showed the pale skin of her back. The boy had sticky-pointy hair and a wide leather belt. A backpack sat beside him, but it wasn't like the man's. Olive moved toward it, though, her heart beating, as if staring at this new, khaki bag would transform it into the man's old, gray one.

The boy looked at her over his girlfriend's shoulder. « Hey, little girl, what do you want? » he asked.

« Have you...has either of you seen a man around here? A dark-haired monsieur with a beat-up backpack? »

« What do you want with this man and his backpack? »

« Nothing... » Olive didn't know what to say. They were squatting his place. Maybe he wasn't far, but she wasn't supposed to go beyond the firethorn. Then she spotted it: a newspaper-wrapped lump under the bench.

« Excuse me, » she said to the two high school kids, kneeling down abruptly in front of the bench and stretching out her arm to grab the package. Her name was scrawled on it, spelled right, the way she'd written it for the man: OLIVE DAVENPORT. She snatched the newspaper and held it to her chest.

« It was someone...a foreign monsieur...he wanted to go to England. » She was still on her knees beside the boy and girl, clutching the small packet.

They were both looking at her now.

« *Un clandestin*? » the girl asked. An illegal?

« What's an illegal? »

« A refugee, one who sneaked in, » the girl told her. « The police cleaned up last night. They put them all on a coach for I don't know where. Some of them are going to ask for asylum in France. Others are going back to where they came from. »

« Back home? » Olive's voice caught.

« So what? What is it to you? »

« Then, they won't be going to England? » asked Olive. Already she could feel the rush of tears behind her eyes, pressing against them like a curtain of oncoming rain.

The girl shrugged and looked at the boy. « Probably not. England doesn't want them. »

They watched her take off like an arrow, dash past the ardent hedge of prickly bush, look both ways.

In the refuge of her bedroom, Olive unfolded the sheets of newspaper with care. Over and over she rubbed Sorayya's slender bracelet between her palms, pressing her nose to the warm metal smell. Then she put it away, ever so carefully, between two leaves of the album where she kept the photographs of Daddy and AH-liv, bouncing on his knee, riding on his shoulders.

Elves

The Icelandic au pair arrived on the one-thirty train. Peter was there to meet her with Mary-Grace, Mary-Veronica, and Mary-Virginia. Mary-Elizabeth and Mary-Margaret stayed at home with their mother, Katie Marie. The Icelandic au pair's hair was long and so blond, it was almost white. She was as tall and strong-looking as a Viking maiden out of the Middle Ages, and Peter felt sure they'd made the right decision in having her come. Katie Marie was at the end of her tether, as Peter would say. She was expecting their sixth child, and the others were all under ten. How could she cope? She couldn't even lift Mary-Margaret; the doctor had strictly forbidden it.

Peter looked over his shoulder at the au pair on the back seat with Mary-Veronica and Mary-Virgina (Ronny and Ginny) on either side of her. Mary-Grace was allowed to sit up front with Daddy, on condition she buckled up, naturally. At present, she was craning backward, straining to see behind her. "Don't stare, girls," Peter told them. "You'll have plenty of time to get acquainted with…Sigridur." He had no idea how to say the young woman's name. She showed no reaction when he pronounced it—he must have been pretty far off base.

"Beg pardon," he said, a little bolder. "Could you tell us how you say your name?"

The girl grinned and repeated something that sounded like "s-thur-thur." Then she added, "But just call me Sigga."

"Fine," said Peter. "Sigga it will be. We were pleased to read on your application that you like children so much."

"Oh, yes," she said airily, "I've been baby-sitting forever--since I was twelve. In America, this is the first time."

ࣿ

Katie Marie explained to Sigga how to make the girls' afternoon snack, and Peter showed her the books she could read them: *Peter Rabbit, Saint Theresa of Lisieux: Little Flower of Jesus, The Christmas Story, The Life of Saint Bernadette, The Little Engine that Could.* He thought he saw the girl frown ever so slightly, but he couldn't be sure. She simply nodded. The children took her upstairs to show her the twins' room. Ronny and Ginny had the largest bedroom in the gray Victorian frame house, and they all gathered there to play. Thanks to a large bay window, there was room for an altar with a statue of Our Lady of Lourdes in her white robe and blue sash. The man at the consignment shop had said it came all the way from the south of France.

Peter had been three months shy of his perpetual vows, when he'd given up the priesthood to marry Katie Marie. Then the little girls had come, first one, then two together, then another and yet another. This time, and with no sexist prejudices, of course, they were truly hoping for a little boy, a dear little Gabriel (namesake to the archangel).

At dinner that evening, Peter noticed the tiny gold cross wedged in Sigga's plunging decolletage. He tried to keep his eye on the cross and not get lost in the geographic splendor of cleavage, which, he was forced to recognize, evoked twin hills so snowy-white, they could have been glaciers. Iceland: land of fire and ice.

"Icelanders are mostly Lutherans?" he inquired politely.

"Yes," she replied. "Traditionally, we're Christians, but you might say that nature is our cathedral. When we're in need of comfort, we don't go to church. We go out into the country."

"Ah." He wasn't quite sure what to make of this. Nature was God's handiwork, however. It couldn't be a bad thing.

The children clambered up to Sigga's made-over attic room for a bedtime story. Peter and Katie Marie heaved a sigh of relief. In eight years of marriage, they hadn't had more than nine months of such peace and quiet.

ࣿ

For the life of him, Peter couldn't recall what he'd done with his missal. Always, but always, he left it on his reading desk, in the upper right-hand corner. The oddest thing was that it turned up in the wheelbarrow full of the leaves he'd raked. If he hadn't dumped them into a pile to be burned, he'd never have noticed it, and its fine leather binding could have rotted away into compost. He questioned each child in turn, but each opened wide, innocent eyes. "Perhaps one of you could ask Sigga," he suggested. He didn't dare confront her with something so uncanny. How could he possibly insinuate she might be responsible for throwing the missal into the autumn leaves? But the thought nagged at the back of his mind.

Gracie (Mary-Grace) reported back from Sigga. "She says it might be the elves," Gracie chirped, as if this were a logical deduction anyone could have made.

"Elves? What ideas has she been putting into your heads? Elves do not exist." Peter was adamant and not at all pleased. Moreover, Sigga was making fun of him.

"Yes, Daddy, they do," Gracie confirmed. "Sigga says she brought some in her suitcase with her from Iceland."

"Well, tell her to send them back on the next plane." Peter tried to joke, but he was not amused. I'll have to speak to Sigga, he thought.

He put it off. In fact, he was quite frightened she would find him ridiculous. Sigga had such a fey, mischievous way of looking at him, with her head lowered, her blue eyes laughing, and the corners of her mouth upturned. It made him uncomfortable and enchanted him all at once.

A week later, Lizzie (Mary-Elizabeth) fell ill, with a burning fever and a rigidity to the nape of her neck that sent Katie Marie to the telephone in a panic. Take her to Emergency immediately, the pediatrician ordered. The sick child cried and demanded Sigga.

Tests and examinations revealed a stiff neck and a touch of the flu: nothing dangerous. Lizzie could go home. Still she wailed, until her parents finally gave permission for her to lie on Sigga's bed in the attic. After an hour, Sigga carried the calmly sleeping Lizzie in her pale, strong arms down to the child's own bedroom. Her little forehead was as cool as a maple leaf and her head wobbled ever so slightly on her relaxed, sweetly curving neck.

"There's something about this I don't like," Peter confided to Katie Marie.

"That you don't like? Our child is well! What does it matter if Sigga calmed her and not you or I or the nurses at the hospital? "

"I'm afraid she's recited some sort of formula, performed some Norse rite—a *pagan* rite. I tell you, there's something preternatural about that girl."

"Peter! And you, such a believer—if the rite were pagan, it couldn't work! Perhaps Sigga is a bit of a saint, then? The girls certainly adore her. They spend hours listening to her stories. Icelandic folklore, she says she tells them. It can't hurt."

For the first time, Peter heard music coming from the attic room. They'd left no radio up there, but perhaps Sigga had a CD player. He knocked shyly at the door. As usual, his troupe of daughters sat in a circle around their baby-sitter. She was bent over a flat, harp-like instrument decorated with some manner of nordic glyphs, Celtic-looking curlicues and symbols he didn't recognize. She sang in a soft, low voice, murmuring sounds he didn't recognize either. To his surprise, the girls joined in, in chorus. They were singing in Icelandic. He felt drawn into the circle, mesmerized. "Come sit with us," Sigga said, smiling obliquely. "You can learn the words, too."

"Oh, no, no thank you," Peter stammered. Sigga's platinum braids were like ropes, drawing him in, her eyes like wells of cool, lagoon-blue water. He nearly tripped, running down the stairs, and thought he heard his own girls laughing at him.

When he began to hear thumping and giggling in the night, Peter started to fear for his sanity. Katie Marie swore up and down she'd never heard anything, and Heaven knew she was a light sleeper, what with heartburn from the baby and the constant pressure on her bladder. She was up every two hours, and there wasn't any thumping, let alone giggling. He was having dreams, just meaningless dreams.

Afraid once more of appearing foolish, Peter dropped the subject, but when the sounds came again, he rose on tiptoe and stood at the bottom of the attic stairs. A gentle hand on his shoulder made him whirl around in terror.

"It's just me," said Sigga, with what he took for a smirk. " I've been for a glass of water," and indeed, she was carrying a half-filled glass. Her hand descended his arm in a stroking motion (or so it seemed), and as she smiled again, her eyes screwed into an amused slant. "Sleep well," she cooed. "Don't let the elves get you."

A little later that same night, Katie Marie's water broke. Peter helped her into the car, leaving the children in Sigga's care. When he got home at eight in the morning, pale and exhausted, he was the proud father of a minuscule archangel. Katie Marie was to stay three days in the maternity ward.

Sigga took over the household with ease. The children obeyed her at a glance; even baby Mary-Margaret (Meggie) played quietly in her playpen without ever whining for her mommy. Peter slid into bed the first evening, missing Katie Marie's rotund presence. As he laid his head on the pillow, something hard and cold met his cheek. He snapped the bedside lamp back on and looked: it was a small, finely wrought key. He felt anger welling inside him. She was going too far—leaving the key to her bedroom on his pillow! He would have to make himself clear; he was not interested in playing games. Peter bounded out of bed and bolted up the attic stairs, only to stop short in front of Sigga's room. No light seeped from under the door. Could she be asleep? He wasn't sure it was the key to her room: he had no recollection of there ever being a key. He felt his resolution wane. He would just test the door to see if it were locked. If it was, then surely she'd left the key for him. If not… He turned the doorknob ever so slowly, silently… the door gave; the room was pitch dark. He pulled the door shut as quietly as he could and tiptoed back down the stairs like a thief, his cheeks burning with embarrassment no one could see. He made up his mind to leave the key by Sigga's coffee cup in the morning. He hardly slept, but not for excitement over his newborn son.

"This is odd," Sigga exclaimed, noticing the key, as she picked up her steaming mug. "It's the key to my suitcase. However did it get here?"

Peter kept his eyes on the formica table top. Finally, the silence and Sigga's (feigned?) puzzlement became too much for him, and he blurted out: " I found this on my pillow last night." He tried to keep the blame out of his voice, but it was there in spite of him.

"Aha! One of my elves, for sure," she said. "They're so afraid I'll shut them in again—they want to be certain I don't have the key any more." Then she tossed her blond head, and Peter was quite sure she'd blinked slyly at him.

"Sigga, really…elves, fairies, trolls…they make charming stories for children, but surely you don't believe they really exist?"

"Isn't this proof?" she asked, matter-of-factly. "In Iceland, I can assure you, they exist."

On the second evening of Katie Marie's hospitalization, Peter returned after visiting hours to find the house empty—or so it seemed at first sight. He found the children, however, gathered in the twins' room around Sigga, playing Chinese checkers. Sigga held Meggie on her lap, and Lizzie was snuggled between her legs. What magnetism did she possess, that they played so quietly, were so good, so uncomplaining? He didn't hear their usual bickering, the running, the cries—or even, in fact, their laughter. Had she hypnotized them?

"Time for bed now, girls," he announced and clapped his hands. They got up so promptly, he wondered why he'd clapped his hands.

Sigga carried Meggie off, with Lizzie in tow.

Half an hour later, she joined Peter in front of the television. The sound seemed to go down of itself, as she sat beside him. He was imagining it, of course. Every time Sigga was near, he began imagining things. The swelling in his trousers, for example: surely, that was not taking place. He willed it not to.

Sigga turned toward him and remarked, "American TV is silly. Why not turn it off?" She snatched the remote control and the screen went blank. Then she turned and looked him squarely in the eye. "What are you afraid of, Peter?" she asked. "Elves don't hurt people. They just play tricks and tease." She ran her hand up his thigh until it met the unseemly bump above his crotch. The golden cross dangled in her V-neck, as she bent towards his fly. Peter took a deep breath and let her undo the button, pull down the zipper. *Know ye not that the unrighteous shall not inherit the kingdom of God? Be not deceived: neither fornicators, nor idolaters, nor adulterers…* He was paralyzed. A sorceress--she must be a sorceress, he thought helplessly.

Katie Marie returned home to find the new au pair already settled in. She was a robust, auburn-haired girl from the Irish countryside, plump, freckled, as wholesome as freshly-baked soda bread. Peter had explained how Sigga'd been called home by her family, oh, so unexpectedly. Luckily, the Association had someone just waiting for a position. She was from County Cork, and her name was Mary-Kathleen.

As Peter wheeled the cradle into the twins' room (they'd have to share with Gabriel for the time being), he caught sight of Our Lady of Lourdes in her niche. He turned and looked a second time. She'd winked at him; he could have sworn she had.

Rummage Sale

It began as a small slip of paper with my name and address on it, buried in the woolly depths of a jacket pocket, as if forgotten. I had begun doing this the way dreamers stuff messages into bottles and toss them into the ocean. The ocean, however, swallows much of what it gobbles up, and its shores are countless, whereas my little papers had a sure destination, Romania or Poland the most often, sometimes Armenia, where rubble from the earthquake still litters the circumference of broken houses.

It wasn't because I wanted to be thanked. I liked the images I created in my mind of tentative fingers, a man's or a woman's, little matter, seeking the warmth of that pocket. Meeting the crumpled paper, their owner, intrigued, would pull it out, contemplate the foreign name, turn it every which way, spell out the letters, call, « Hey, look, here is the name of our benefactor. This was in the pocket. It's a woman's name, probably. ' Lisa.' That would be a woman, wouldn't it? From America. From O-h-i-o. » I liked to imagine them trying to say « Ohio, » trying to recall where it might be, long-time-ago geography lessons, fantasies of the promised land.

I didn't really expect answers either. People in the thrall of distress or misery need food, warmth, and clothes, not pen-pals. However, should there be one person, only one, in search of friendship too, I was ready to tender that along with the rest. The clothes I folded into packages for the charities that sent them were woven vehicles of affection, special delivery vans of consideration, crossing the earth.

Second-hand clothes are special and rummage sales intriguing. You may have noticed the odor that floats above the turnover table in the church basement: a mixture of other women's armpits and stale deodorant. My own clothes huddled together in the closet do not produce that indefinable, animal aroma that everyone else's together invariably exhale. But it can be coaxed away. A good wash, old-fashioned drying in sun and wind, a steam iron for the bacteria, and, if necessary, drench it in your favorite perfume and put it in the draft again.

After that, the fibers can begin soaking *you* up. I love this appropriation of another's finery, especially when I can buy it for a song. Delving into the pile of cast-offs, combing, scouring until the desirable, the unexpected, the unforeseen bargain appears among the waste is like a game with no losing score.

Depending on the degree of social snobbery of my interlocutors, I either brag about these little finds in answer to compliments or gloss over them. One woman I know washes or dry-cleans any brand new garment she buys before wearing it. When I asked her why one day, my question evoked a raised eyebrow. « Someone *else* might have *tried it on*! » This should have been plain to the meticulous person I obviously was not. Hygiene or neurosis?

If I wash my second-hand treasures, I also enjoy altering them when necessary, remaking them to redefine them as mine. Until I tire of them in turn and prepare them for their next life in a Care package or a Red Cross package, off to the denizens of despair that people our planet. With discreet strips of paper, stashed in pockets like grocery lists.

« Dear *Pani* Lisa, » the letter began. It was entirely written in Polish of which I do not speak a word. I invested in a fat Polish-English dictionary and worked my way through the page, laborious word by laborious word, boggled by declensions and conjugations, relieved just to discover, when I could, the roots of the nouns and verbs and suck some of the sap of meaning from them. The inhabitual consonant clusters, the extra alphabet letters with their little dots and slashes and buttonhook tails, created a foreign landscape where I travelled an unsure but exotic road, one that breathed out the smoke of woodfires and factory chimney stacks and yielded up rocky hurdles of meaning: *collective, nationalized, privatized, closed, unemployment, invalid, pension, scholarship, refusal.*

Alicja had a chronic illness and was waiting for a decision on her disability pension. Eugeniusz, her husband, had found no job once his State-subsidized factory had been closed by order of the new government, and he was falling into depression. Jacek, in his last term of high school, would be taking his national examination, the *matura*, at the end of the year. His older sister, Katarzyna, was learning to be a nurse. She had loved the blazer, so Western, so elegant. She was very sorry her English was inadequate. Here were some words of German she knew. The shoe and clothing sizes of the whole family.

I did not wait until the next jumble sale but bought new sneakers for the two young people. I gathered chocolate, coffee, canned foods, and a variety of garments that I wrapped in old sheets of the local newspaper. I primped and pressed them lovingly and thought to put small treats in the pockets.

Brimming with good intentions, I drove my unwieldy package to the Polish travel agency. They specialized in mailing to Poland; this information was plastered on their front windows.

The receptionist spoke to me in the swishing, shushing sounds of her native language, and I pointed to my carton. She in turn showed me the room behind her, empty except for a huge scale.

Another non-English speaker, an elderly man this time in a sleeveless undershirt, appeared on the scene, seized the huge box and placed it on the scale. He looked at the address, wrote down a price, and gave me a form to fill in: *odbiorca*, sender, *nadawca,* recipient; *nazwa artykulu*, where I had to list the contents. Then he held up six fingers and pronounced mashed potato syllables, which I took to mean six weeks. Everyone nodded and smiled, and I felt glad my package was already in Polish hands.

Two months later another airmail envelope arrived with its foreign stamp, the address carefully printed in light-blue, ball-point ink. Inside I found a Sears advertisement from my own local newspaper, cut and pasted onto the slightly yellowed stationery. Would I please acquire this power chain saw, it asked, for Eugeniusz? If he had such a marvelous tool, he could get piecework cutting down trees. The forests in their region were great and numerous. And the price of this American marvel was cheaper than anything that could be found in their country. In the envelope, they said, were 100 Deutsche marks they had saved and wished to devote to this purchase. If it wasn't enough, I would please let them know.

I wondered if I had understood correctly; there was a sheet of inky black carbon paper in the envelope, but no money. I wondered a fleeting instant if they had done this on purpose. They would have placed the carbon in the enevelope to make me think they were concealing money but then conveniently forgot the bills.

I looked more closely at the envelope and saw how one side had been opened, then meticulously re-sealed with glue. I felt ashamed for suspecting them. How naïve they had been, how watchful the postal worker! No doubt, the more opaque the envelope, the more eye-catching it would be. I imagined there must be special, strong lamps for this. But why had the employee bothered to repair and glue back the envelope?

Ah, but a State postal worker would never steal news, a personal message, love from family to family - only money, and that because he needed it. And if one was so foolish as to send DMarks around in flimsy envelopes, what could you expect...? Surely the money wasn't so imporant to you, was it?

I weighed telling them this mishap, then thought better of it. I went to Sears and purchased the closest model to the one in the paper that I could find. The stock advertised, of course, had long been sold out.

What would I be needing it for, exactly, asked the salesman.

I didn't mention the forests of Olsztyn. I padded the package with paper toweling this time and slipped inside a letter in simple, schoolgirl German that one of the children should be able to decipher. I added my photograph.

« She is very elegant, our American friend, Lisa, » I imagined them saying. « So young, she looks. » I supposed I was their age, although I felt sure my comfortable American life had preserved me from showing it. I too could have been the mother of children the same ages as Eugeniusz and Alicja's, if fate hadn't denied me that satisfaction.

The young people closest to me were the ones who came into the library where I worked. I loved watching them bent over their school reports, hearing them giggle and whisper over the glazed pages of the heavy encyclopedia volumes. When I lost my husband at thirty-five from an unforeseeable coronary, I lost my hopes of a family too. I would so have liked one or the other of these teenagers to be mine, to come home after his day at school and tell me tales of teachers and baseball games and buddies and crushes. If teenagers do that, that is.

As it was, I returned to my quiet house and studied *Polish in 90 Lessons and 90 Days.*

❧

Jacek had not done well during his first year in auto mechanics. It did not correspond to what he really wanted to do, they wrote.

And what was that, I inquired, but the reply was vague.

He had more intellectual aspirations, Alicja seemed to say. He would have liked to become a writer, a journalist. But his father said a man had to eat. Eugeniusz insisted that his son learn something « useful. » I could feel the conflict, and it pained me. They could not force Jacek to a manual trade if such was not his inclination. I thought how awkward I was with my own hands, whereas books or a pen found their rightful place there. Suddenly an idea dawned in my mind like the opening of a canopy onto a vista of light.

Eugeniusz would not, could not pay for his son to « waste » time on the tomfoolery of literature or languages. I could, however. My own son, if I had had one, would have been enrolled in a liberal arts college, with four leisurely years devoted to acquiring general culture and self-knowledge. Why should I not offer that opportunity to Jacek? He could live with me, study at the nearby community college. That would be easier on my budget than regular college and easier, no doubt, for them to accept. The best, in fact, would be to avoid the question entirely and let them assume it was free public education. As with the power saw, what would they ever know? America, a cornucopia of plenty, is it not? As everyone knows.

If he succeeded, the final two years for his degree could be pursued elsewhere. We would have plenty of time to think about that. I made an appointment with the dean of the college.

A foreign student would be a novelty at his institution and a source of enrichment for the others, the dean assured me. He would, of course, need Jacek's school file from Poland. He gave me the application forms, a brochure, the inevitable financial guarantee sheet to complete. Jacek would need a student visa, which would prevent him from getting an after-school job, although there were some campus jobs available. These were permitted.

My simple German and beginner's Polish would not suffice to explain all this to the family or to convince them. I typed a long, touching (I thought) and persuasive petition in English, then went in search of a translator.

Next to the Polish travel agency, where the packages took off, was a small shop run by frowning Ukrainians, whose idea of commerce was residuary Communist-era. They eyed customers with suspicion, offered no help, and showed annoyment when disturbed with a request for purchase. Their shop-window boasted the Eastern European « chic » of polyester blouses in impossible, acid colors, wide hair-ribbons, and imitation leather shoes in the fashion of ten years previous. Near the blouses stood incongruous piles of somber books with hard, navy blue covers and titles embossed in gold Cyrillic capitals, small household appliances, a bric-à-brac of hardware items.

I felt totally out of place there and had not often dared step beyond the threshold. The door, itself, however, was of considerably more interest than the window display. A bulletin board of little ads and flyers announced the annual picnic of the Friends of the Ukraine (this in English and Russian, or was it Ukrainian?), Russian lessons (native speaker, reasonable price), a second-hand stove for sale (excellent condition), translation services for all Slavic languages...

I wrote down this last telephone number, and then, to celebrate, crossed the street to the Russian delicatessen. Here, if I was intimidated, it was by the bounty and luxury of the foodstuffs spread in refrigerated, glass cases in front of the long counter: square, aluminum containers of salads in white or pink sauces, plump, filled pastries, all shape and species of marinated fish. A large wooden barrel held fat pickles in brine. Near the cash register, small red tins of caviar with black and gold lettering were piled in expensive pyramids.

A buxom, dark-haired girl in a wide, white apron, her black curls gathered in a heavy bouquet on the nape of her neck, presided over the feast. Although she spoke Russian to the customers, her black eyes and olive skin suggested the Caucasus. She served me smoky Russian tea and blinis at a small, round wooden table, and I thought how I would come here later with Jacek on the days he felt nostalgic for things Eastern.

The rest of the time, he would drink Coke with the kids and learn to feel at home in the new world. Would he lie about his age like the others for a beer at the tavern? A Pole would certainly find our drinking laws silly and repressive. I smiled to imagine his reaction.

To sway his parents' final decision, I wired the money for the trip. For a fleeting moment, I wondered if I were buying a ready-made son, but put the idea out of my mind. In fact, I would surely be disappointed. I told myself this day and night. I had to steel myself for it. First of all, Jacek would be ugly. He would be puny and have bad, grayish teeth that had never been properly cared for. Perhaps he would have acne, but, no, that was a plague for the better-fed. His features would be disharmonious and his movements ungainly. Second, he would not be nearly as intelligent as his mother believed. His English would be atrocious and his motivation for learning questionable. He would have a bad temper and bad breath.

At the airport, I held his name against my chest on a rectangular, white card, and he greeted me with a wide hug and a resounding « *czesc!* » which, my book says, is « hi » in Polish. It doesn't sound the way it looks when written. *Czesc,* spoken by a tall young man with broad shoulders, sea-green eyes, and hair the color of honey made from heather, sounds a great deal better than it looks. Jacek radiated strength and self-composure, along with a white, healthy smile: a superb specimen of Slavic humanity. Tears of joy and relief rose to my eyes. I adopted him in the instant. God was my witness. I had done the right thing.

The first snapshot I sent to Alicja and Eugeniusz shows their son at one of his favorite activities: leaning over his plate, delving into the juicy redness of a thick steak. Just watching Jacek eat filled me with the pride of borrowed motherhood. Yes, I could feed this strapping youth and meet his needs.

Turning toward him with dish towel in hand, I awaited his grin when the plate had been emptied, the hot coffee downed.

« Thanks, Aunt Lisa! »

Language, too, I fed him daily. The community college offered no special course for non-native English speakers, but Jacek was enrolled in remedial English, and we reviewed vocabulary and sentence structure together.

His English teacher, Gerald, was helpful and studiously attentive. He started coming to the house, first on the pretext of tutoring Jacek. Later, however, it seemed to matter little to him that Jacek was often not at home for his visits. We talked about « our boy » and his progress or his difficulties, then other things, until our own lives and histories were cautiously, then more confidently, brought out for discussion and sharing.

I had my auburn hair cut in a short, lilting style and started paying attention to the women's magazines I usually scorned, with their tips on make-up and other strategies of seduction. Maroon lispstick was the thing that fall season, and I discovered that if I first outlined my lips in dark red, then filled in with the brownish burgundy, they looked pulpy and appetizing.

My co-workers complimented me, and the people I met daily, mailman, grocery cashier, neighbor, suddenly seemed to see me. If Gerald did not stop by after class, I felt a twinge of disappointment that I shook off when Jacek, sweaty from soccer, would cry out « *cesc*! » and bound down the hall to the shower.

Calls often came for him on his cell phone, my present for his nineteenth birthday. Sometimes I heard him speaking English, but, more often, and this puzzled me, Polish. I asked him nothing, however. I was Aunt Lisa, neither mother-hen nor eavesdropper, and his fleeting presence in the house sufficed to swell my heart.

Before the first term was over, I tried discussing his future plans with him, but he was evasive, and the subject did not seem to interest him. He needed time to adapt, to enjoy himself, to learn English and make friends. What plans do most youngsters have at nineteen? I would not rush Jacek but let him soak up America. And I would savor that time.

I asked Alicja to describe a Polish Christmas for me. I had to get it right, prevent too much homeward yearning. I would make the beet broth and stuff the carp. I told him we would invite any school friends he wished for Christmas Eve, but he simply smiled at me.

« Just you is fine, » he said. « Maybe you want Gerald, I mean Mr. King, to come too? »

I decided I did. I needed the red velvet dress I had seen in a shop window that afternoon, too. It was a sheath with long sleeves and a square neckline. I had noticed how the material folded gracefully across the bust.

Jacek's phone rang, and he galloped off to his room to talk. I heard muffled Polish.

For once I would not be at my sister's for Christmas but would make my own celebration. A dark pine stood in splendor in one corner, and I had placed decorated candles in every nook and corner of the living room. A waxy, piney small filled the air, and the glow from the candles made vacillating shadows.

At six on Christmas Eve, Gerald rang the bell, a pile of packages in his arms. « Just some little remembrances for you and Jacek, » he said.

We would open them after the Christmas Eve Mass. Neither he nor I were Catholics, but we had decided to accompany Jacek to Mass. His mother had said it was indispensable.

I had one or two little things to do in the kitchen, and then we could begin. Three porcelain cups of creamy egg nog waited on a tray. On the table was my best white, damask tablecloth and, in the middle, in a crystal dish, lay the traditional Communion wafer Alicja had sent, for faith and sharing and home. I had also laid the extra place for the wayfarer and was eager to see Jacek's response to my attempts at Polish custom. I would just go to his room and get him.

I knocked on the door, but there was no answer. After several knocks, I opened the door a crack, then wider, expecting to see my Jacek dozing on his bed. The bed was neatly made and the room empty. Not just empty of Jacek, but empty of his belongings as well. An eerie quiet lay over everything. I noticed the fine film of dust on the bedside table, and the dark, shiny round where his electronic alarm clock had been.

My heart beating too quickly, I looked in the closet. The scuffed, black suitcase he had brought from Poland was there, but his backpack was gone and about half of his clothes.

Dazed, I sat on the bed and scanned the room. His cell phone, radio, and CD player were missing too. There was no message of any kind. Where could he have gone? Where could he afford to go?

Seized with sudden panic, I ran to look at my cash drawer in the kitchen: empty. It had been cleaned out of the $300 I knew was in it. That would not take him to Poland but would get him quite far on a Greyhound. Or would he hitchhike and use it for something else? I told myself it was a hallucination and that in a moment he would be back, laughing, wishing us a merry Christmas.

Gerald saw my distress and came to ask what was wrong. I collapsed in his arms, unable to get a single word out.

On Christmas Day, I phoned the translator of my letter. She would have to call their parish priest, I told her, who would go and get the family. They had no telephone.

The priest would have Masses to celebrate on Christmas Day, what could one expect, she said. And the phone lines buzzed with overburdening. A recording in Polish repeated this to us over and over.

We didn't get through to Jacek's parents until the following day. Alicja and Eugeniusz were surprisingly unconcerned. He must have had business, they said: « *Beez-ness* ». Something about it sounded shady and unscrupulous. I was not to worry, and they thanked me for everything. They hung up very quickly.

Jacek had taken his new, American tee shirts, sweatshirts, and jeans but left his Polish clothes. In February, I placed these in the carton I was preparing for the spring rummage sale at the church. I also folded the splendid new sweater I had planned to give him for Christmas, one of those ecru Irish cable knits, and added it to the pile. I put in my red velvet dress, too, for this year's Christmas had not been one I would want to remember. Someone else could use it, would delight in finding it, would alter it, perhaps, and make it hers. Insfoar as she could, I mean. Make it hers.

Mirror

Mitrovica, Kosovo. My husband's name is Donat, and he has half a face. The Serbs took the other half, took it with one of their bullets, at the same time they took my brother's life. My husband's face, my brother's life, and here am I, Feti, with this huge belly and a child kicking inside it, kicking to get out into this confused and vicious world of ours. Rejoice in the new life, they tell me, but how, how can I rejoice, when my child will be born to a father with half a face?

I'll tell you how it happened, if you can bear it. It was raining, April rain, the kind that brings mud and mold and the flu sometimes. This year it brought the paramilitaries with their torches: Milan, for one; I went to high school with him, and Drago, my grandmother's neighbor. I didn't know the others.

They never saw me, how I hid behind the manure pile and escaped through the prune orchard. I'm slight and dark, and, even five months pregnant, I was fleet like a fawn.

Donat wasn't at home when they came, but he saw the flames from the hill where Adhurim's windmill spins the breeze. When the fire fizzled out in the rain, he looked through the ashes and knew I could never have been at the house. He walked all the way to the village, three kilometers, with Rexhep and Faruk, my brothers.

They all thought I was there, at Auntie's, but I wasn't. I was still in our neighborhood, in the run-down barn near the crossroads, but how could they have known that?

The Serbs were at the village now, too, moving in rings like the circles of hell closing in. They had on black hoods to hide the shame of what they were doing, but evil can never be anonymous. They had it in for every Albanian who breathed in that village, and young men were their targets of choice.

Donat is a young man, and I married him for love. I married him because I wanted to sleep with him, and it was the only way. It's not our custom, sleep before marriage. I let him touch the warm place sometimes, just with his fingers when he kissed me, but I wanted more. I needed him to fill me, to take up all the hungry space.

We're only twenty-two, both of us, and he hasn't even finished school yet. My mother said, your young man ought to complete his diploma first, but my father said, let them get married! Otherwise, they'll be disgracing us, so hurry it up! I want my daughter married in a white gown, and her honor intact.

On our wedding day, I had three strings of pearls around my neck and three more in my hair, which is black. It was piled on my head with the veil attached in back, and I had strands of curls spilling around my face like party festoons.

Donat was as serious as a judge, and tears came into his eyes when he made his promise. On our wedding photograph, you can see how earnest he is, with his eyes dark like strong coffee and his nose so straight and narrow. He isn't smiling, but his mouth is very beautfiul just as it is, not sensuous but kind and firm, the mouth of a strong-willed man.

I say very beautiful, but that was until the bullets, of course. One stung Rexhep in the leg, but he kept running. Pain is nothing, when you are nineteen, and your life is at stake. The other reached Faruk's heart, and he will run no longer. As for Donat, I've told you; the bullet they shot at him splintered away half his face, that face I loved.

He was running towards the wood when they caught sight of him, and the impact and the searing felled him in a second. He must have passed out; he doesn't remember, only suddenly the sound of boots around him, pounding the damp earth so it vibrated. He never moved.

God, let them think I am dead, he prayed, and they did.

He let an eternity of time go by, maybe one hour, maybe two. Only death could be more silent than the village was then. Had they even slaughtered the chickens in the poultry runs and the hunting dogs tied to their posts?

Donat got up slowly, tentatively. The ground spun up to meet him, and his stomach rose and lapped against his insides in waves. The wood appeared to him through a grey curtain of fog. One eye seemed to be out of commission, but he could see that his shirt was sticky with blood, could still feel it trickling. There was no pain, only an odd pulling on one side of his face and too much sensitivity to the chill in the air.

The rain had stopped some time before.

For two nights and two days, my husband lay low in that wood with his wound gaping. He never knew how cruel the damage was. Had he known, he would have let himself die, people said afterwards.

It's just my teeth; my teeth are broken, he thought, but his fingertips told him they were all there. What was the bony material he felt then? God preserved him from knowing it was his own smashed cheek and nose, for there is no reflection in bark and pine needles.

He came to a large puddle, lay down in front of it and sucked in great throatfuls. The rainwater was cold and pure, and mercifully it kept its secret. No Narcissus he, Donat did not look when he backed away from it. The surface was flat and silvery like the mirror in the hall of my father's house.

I will not look, he thought, turning away his gaze. I do not want to know. I will find out in due time.

When the sun had set and risen twice, he left the wood. He knows our villages by heart, Donat does, and the people know him: the farmhand's son who's at the university in Pristina, the one who got married last October. A sunny day it was and a beautiful couple.

They never thought the ogre coming from the wood could be the same one, oh no, not he. His face was blood and gore, no longer a human face, God help us, and the children ran away.

Old man Saladin is afraid of nothing, though. He has seen horrors in his day, and he took Donat's arm with commiseration. He looked at our wedding picture. Donat pulled it from the back pocket of his jeans. He kept it there for luck, always, an amulet you might say, a happy reflection. He still does.

« Allah! Is that who you are, boy? Ali's son? » When he realized that they didn't recognize him, Donat began to guess the extent of it.

I fainted when they brought him to me, and it was just as well. We had not been sure if he was dead or alive, but we knew they hadn't found his body. We'd buried Faruk already, but I was waiting for Donat to come back to me. The child turned in my belly and brought me to myself. The creature with half his head gouged and gashed was my husband, they told me.

I was at Auntie's by then, and the KFOR had arrived in the village. They had gauze and disinfectant. When I really came to, the pulp and destruction were hidden behind a white veil of bandages.

God, why not his arm, why not his leg, why this part of him that is so much You? Can You still see Yourself in him, *can* You?

We have cared for him for two months' time now. It is my mother and Auntie who dress the wound. I am ashamed to say so, but I cannot bring myself to do it. We are all piled into what remains of her cinder block house, and it is dank and unhealthy. Infection could run rampant here, but it does not. He is condemned to get well. Donat is very brave, very determined.

« I will be myself again for you, Feti, » he promises.

How can that ever be, I think, but I keep those thoughts to myself.

He has begun going to a clinic on the outskirts of the town, a charity clinic, set up by an American, tall and hefty, the way they make them there. I tell him to stop hoping, but he won't let go. They speak of America, of England. We have no money for operations abroad, I say, but Donat keeps the faith.

« Don't let the doctor tell you they can do something, » I say. Hope is too terrifying to me.

Manchester, England. Medical science has wrought a miracle, they tell us. Now there is skin across the gap that was once my husband's martyred face. It has been fleshed in with fat from his own body; built up with false bones and cartilage from his own ear. A ribbon of skin crosses over where the bridge of his nose should be. They will repair the eye socket, they say. In the meantime, leave the patch of bandage. His face is purple and twisted and tumefied, but that is just a matter of time, the doctors reassure us.

Still, my husband does not look at himself in any other mirror than that of my own eyes. Can I lie? Can I tell him, Yes, I know you? You are my own love, the dark young man I married in the sun in October, over there, far away, in a place where war has left only ruins? Where other ruins have not been repaired? What can my eyes tell him? I steel myself and I look, steadily. I clench my hands, and I smile.

It rains in this English city, too, where they've brought us. So much good will, so much generosity, so much skill and devotion in this place where rain falls on red brick and soot.

I must be grateful, but I miss it back there, even the ruins. I miss my life; I miss my love. I live with a gentle young man I cannot recognize. I look at the wedding photograph. I remind myself. I shut my eyes and let him touch the warm place and do my best to believe that it is he.

The child is here now, and we pose with him for newspapers, in honor of the helpful soldiers, and the clever doctors, and the miracle that spared Donat. We have called the child Faruk, for my brother, but it is his father he resembles. He is the true mirror--small, round reflection of God--and his father's healthy eye shines with just the same light as his two. Yes, it is good to have this mirror.

My Daughter, *Ma Mère*

In this country, they rig you out in sheets for modesty: on top, a starched, cotton smock that yawns in the back, and for the rest of you, a wide, white rectangle like a tent over your knees.

"We have to get our feet in the stirrups," the girl says. "Can I help you?"

I try not to grunt, as I raise each limb in turn. Unaided. That "we" of condescension. If I were twenty years younger, would she dare?

"Move closer to the edge of the table. That's it! The doctor will be with you in a minute."

There is an even greater indignity than having someone shove a pink, rubber pessary down your nether parts, oh no--not for the sake of contraception—I'm nearly thirty years beyond any preoccupation of that sort. Mine is to keep my bladder in place, to save me, commonly speaking, from wetness--pardon me, *de l' incontinence*. Insertion is, after all, a medical procedure, and I am not the first seventy-eight-year-old to undergo it. It's been done to younger than I. No, the indignity is in how they summon you in here, in the first place: "*Marguerite?*" My first name, and from a snub-nosed, short-skirted chubby pup of a girl younger than my grandchildren. If I had grandchildren. *Marg-you-reet*, she pronounced it. I could almost have laughed. Yet along with that, they cover you as if your body were by definition shameful—or is it that I'm going to seduce the gynecologist with my pathetic old flaps and folds?

Where I come from, it's *Monsieur le docteur* himself who always came to get me in the waiting room. "*Madame* Lévesque," he'd say. He'd be holding my file. His reading glasses were always half-way down his nose, and he never smiled when he said my name or anyone else's.

When I pointed these differences out to Charlotte, she just said, "*This* country is a real democracy. None of our high and mighty *manières* here."

"Well, and do you call the *doctor* by his first name?" I asked, but she just shrugged at that.

Lord, Maman, quit being such an old crank!

I have been living with Charlotte, my only child, in her new country for three months now. This country is *new* insofar as it's been civilized for a lot less time than our old one, and new *to her* in that she's from the grass roots of western France, like her mother and grandmother before her. It's *hers* through the good graces of her husband, Joe MacMahon.

ChaCha met Joe when she was studying English for a term at a state college in New Jersey, twenty-five years ago already. That's to give you an idea of ChaCha's age. She's reached ripeness, now, and I have to admit, it becomes her. She was such a fey slip of a girl, with that short, brunette hair and the pale oval face—elfin, like Annie Girardot's used to be. America has fed Charlotte in more ways than one: with kilograms and self-confidence. At four, she was still hiding behind my skirts, whenever I'd… But there I go, talking about the past again.

One more rewind to my childhood and I'll explode.

I can just about read her mind a good deal of the time, and I know it irritates her, but what else have people like me got left from the precious time triptych of past-present-future? There's none of the last part for us any more, so we make the best of the other two.

Take Charlotte's wedding to Joe. There, by the way, is the nicest young man you'll ever meet, even if he isn't French. It makes her laugh to hear me say "young," when he's nearing fifty now, but seen from my own Mont Blanc heights, the grass is still very green on the plains around the half-century milestone.

"Marguerite? Hi, I'm Doctor Coleman. If you could just edge up a bit more. This'll only take a second."

Maybe I should feel flattered that he's surely using the same tone with me as with the girl who was here just seconds before. But why should a wizened old piece of fruit like me be dropped into the same basket as a juicy, blushing apple? At least I still have some sort of canal down there, or he wouldn't be able to do his little sleight-of-hand with the pink device.

"*Voilà*!" That's the word where you come from, right?

"Yes, it is," I counter, trying gamely to keep my composure, all the while speaking English and holding up my twin-peaked circus tent. I remember learning, oh, ever so long ago, that you must never say a plain "yes" or just "no." "Yes, it is. No, it isn't." I was always a docile student.

"Now, grab onto your walker—your little Camaro convertible, right? Ha ha!--and when you're dressed, you can join your daughter. She's waiting in my office."

Clop-plonk, shuffle-plonk. Here comes Mother. I know it's despicable of me to reproach her for using that thing, but when I hear it, my skin crawls. It'll be your turn one day, Charlotte, I tell myself, so be charitable. And still, I have to clench my teeth.

"Well, *ma chérie*, I'm outfitted," I say in French. "They tell me it's accident-proof."

She forces a smile. Poor Charlotte. The spectacle of your mother's decline is that of your own, and the reprieve is bound to be short-lived. What's a mere generation, after all? So thin a shield from age and death. If Joe hadn't fallen unemployed, as we say in French, she wouldn't have to subject herself to the sad sight of my decrepitude. But I know what inspired their offer to have me move in with them. If my pension and the income from my Paris apartment were to go to a retirement home, there'd be nothing for them. This way, it's all benefit. How much does an old lady eat, after all? True enough, I ask them to turn the heat up more than they're accustomed, but that's nothing in comparison to what I have brought to the household. In a material sense, of course.

The house is stifling. Why does she never think of airing out her room? I have to do it when her back is turned, or she'll accuse me of wanting her to freeze to death. And the toilet. I guess she never has her glasses on in the bathroom. I read somewhere that we are never repelled by the secretions of those closest to us. I suppose that could be true, but the other way around. A mother can change her baby without a thought, but scrubbing your mother's intestinal wastes off a white, porcelain bowl—patiently, tenderly? Please! And how long must the child heave in labor, giving birth to the mother?

Still, it's not such a price to pay. Joe hasn't found anything, and we'd have lost the house by now.

I remember the first time I saw their home, one of those typical American affairs, all frail wood and picket fence and acidulated-green lawn like a wrap-around skirt. It seemed to spring out of a child's picture album, except that everyone else had the same. Where we come from, a real house is made of stone with walls three feet thick. Even Charlotte has confessed to dreaming, time and again, of limestone cottages with heavy lavender shutters, as if this flimsy matchbox of hers could never afford protection from nightmares, real or imagined.

Little did I think then that I'd be spending my last days in their pastel, dollar-colored playhouse. If I had a jot of common sense, I should consider myself fortunate. How many people my age are left to mold among their peers, ignored if not mistreated? Most, I would guess. We live in selfish times, when aging parents are as disposable as tissues. Which I detest, by the way—you always end up blowing your nose in your fingers--but my Charlotte will use them. "Handkerchiefs are so unhygienic," she gripes. "Ugh, carrying dried snot around in your pocket! That was all right in the Middle Ages."

Joe is not like that, though, not a thrower-away. He calls me "Beautiful Mom"; that's his own literal translation of "*belle-mère,*" mother-in-law. That arm's-length term is undiluted Anglo-Saxon pragmatism: "*ma mère dans la loi.*" The legal chill of it makes me shudder. It's enough to incite us to deserve our reputation as meddling shrews.

Meddle, I do not. Let them live their lives, I say, make their mistakes, claim their own hard-won wisdom. Even if I gave the best advice on two continents, it would be resented—all the more for being good, no doubt. That doesn't mean I don't see things, though. That I don't see Joe's discomfiture when he gets back after another fruitless day tracking jobs. That I don't see Charlotte's shenanigans. Why did she let the cat meow in front of the door to the den yesterday for ten full minutes, then open just a crack? Why did she come home early from work on the sly, then suddenly appear in the front hall at the usual time crying out "Hi!" at the top of her lungs?

Maman is as deaf as a stoneware jug. That suits me just fine, things being what they are, and at the same time, it's indecent, abhorrent. She can't walk properly, can't hear half what I tell her, can't remember what day it is. She used to run, to sing, to recite La Fontaine's Fables and kilometers of verse. I indict this mother for not being that one. The pretty one, the vivacious one whose image I want to stash away intact in my mind. And then I know I've got to stop. As if any of it were her fault.

Joe has put grip bars in the bathroom all around the shower. That's to say how considerate he is. Old people aren't supposed to bathe too often—as if that crackly, parchment skin of ours might rub off, tear away from the blue ropes that stubbornly lug the life-flow. Nonetheless, there's a rancid, tallow smell when I take off my baby-pink bathrobe. I've got to use the place more often, whatever they say. The thing to avoid is the mirror above the sink. I don't know the crone in there. I have thick, chestnut hair and a china-teacup complexion. I have slim, dark eyebrows and a dimple in my left cheek. That woman has a gray mustache and furrows in her face too deep to plow. She frightens me. I don't know her from Eve.

I wish she wouldn't adulate Joe so; it just makes me feel more uncomfortable. She could never understand how that hang-dog expression of his drives me crazy. It's not worthy of a documentary-maker--an artist, as he says. Of course there's no work in that. There are lots of things he could do—beneath him, all right, but he could do them, temporarily. That's the beauty of this society. Upward mobility, but downward, too, just the time your little, personal recession lasts. And nobody points his finger at you. Tough times, they'll say, and they'll understand. Joe's got a stubborn streak and won't settle for less than what he wants, so long as we can hold out. He forgets the emotional attrition. Mine.

Charlotte helps me up the steps. *Fini*, the gynecologist, for three months anyway, until the next oil-change. I can feel her impatience to get away. She's taken time off from her office for me, needs to get back. "I just need to grab my things," she says. "See you later."

She works in real-estate, and her earnings are irregular, at best. The season is slow, the economy morose. Often she's called to show people around some barn or some dollhouse of a place, but they don't seem to be in buying moods these days. It's hard for me to imagine her praising, no less selling, these *petite-maison-dans-la-prairie* constructions, but she has to do something, she says. She got all her training here, learned the business--more power to her. Dealings are different from *chez nous*, but this is all she knows, now. Part of her belongs to this culture, lost to me forever. I have to remember that I'm the foreigner here, not her. Foreign to this country, foreign to my child, foreign, most of the time, to myself. Now I'm the one in training, I say--training for my visa to that vast continent foreign to us all, and from which there's no return ticket.

In the meantime, I would like to know whose key ring that is on the kitchen table, that one, with the plastic Stars and Stripes. Joe's has a scratched-up, jello-green shamrock on it, and ChaCha carries around a red plush puffin that dangles along with the keys. There is no car out front, and I can't hear anything in the house. But then, I never can hear anything. I don't want a hearing-aid that screeches and whistles every time you move your head. Those are fine for old hags. Yes, I know; ears are no place to house your pride. But I've had enough of doctors for a while. I'll see next month, or the month after, or when I can't stand not knowing certain things any longer.

With Joe, I don't need the walker. He gives me his arm and leads me up and down in front of the house. Lift the feet, don't drag them. Watch out for the cracks in the sidewalk. Our little fitness hour, he says. He's solidly built, that fellow. Irish stock. His people came over during the Great Potato Famine, first to Canada, then down here. He's showed me some pictures, definitely more ancient than I! His great-great grandmother has something like an overturned lampshade on her head, and the grandpa looks like a savage from the woods. Joe's no wild man; he's a real gentleman, no matter how poor and famished his people were. The French and the Irish have always been good friends. Or maybe it's that the enemies of my enemies are my friends? No love lost between either of our countries and the English.

He and ChaCha have always made an attractive couple: peasant-strong Joe and fragile, European-elegant Charlotte. What I notice these days is that they don't appear to touch each other any more. Each one's in his own bubble, but they both talk to me. Come to think of it, it would be better if they talked around me or over me or even behind my back. My presence at meals or in the living room doesn't seem to bother them as much as it should.

She's always there. I know you can't blame someone merely for existing, but why must she just always be there? Her walker peeks out from behind the angle her door makes with the hall—a metal harbinger—then, shuffling in her plaid men's slippers, she follows. Her coming, at least, is always heralded.

Well, here's my Joe, now, home already. I know he's dejected, but he always has a smile for Beautiful Mom. Charlotte's more evasive. She's a girl who does her duty by her old *Maman*, but I'd better not ask for more. I suppose Joe's situation gets her down, and, besides, who wants to live with a constant reminder that health and beauty are impermanent attributes?

Joe offers to take me to the backyard. You can walk all around the houses in this neighborhood; none stuck together, no rows. Everyone's got his little barbecue out back, his lawn chairs, sometimes a deck. The weather's warming up, flowers opening out like popcorn. It all reminds me of those *pointilliste* paintings: pink and white dots dazzling your eyes till they smart.

As we get to the back of the house, I catch sight of a sandy-haired man slipping out the side-door. He looks right and left, much as if he were going to cross a street. But there's only the driveway. Then he breaks into a run. Like a robber. Curious. I look questioningly at Joe, but he's frozen in his tracks. "Toby!" he says. "How could… So it's him… Oh, God!"

I've heard Joe mention that name before. Toby. A friend of his.

I get the impression he's going to fade away behind a mask of pallor. Then he pulls himself together, says why not go inside now, why not make a snack, see if Charlotte's home. I nod rigidly. Of course Charlotte's home. I've just caught on. Finally caught on.

I act as if I never noticed anything amiss. Joe stirs hot cocoa for me as though his life depended on it, and I pretend to be interested in watching him. Charlotte makes a show of slamming the front door and calling out to me. That "*Hi*" again, as if she's just walked in. She almost succeeds in converting her surprise at Joe's presence into solicitude. She thought he'd been to Manhattan today, she says, thought he'd had an interview. Over *already*? How lovely! How did it go?

He says it was canceled. He got the first train back. His voice is as crisp as burnt toast. He turns on his heels and walks out of the kitchen.

❧

I didn't much care for the *notaire*'s tone of politely repressed disapproval, when I gave him my instructions, but he has to carry them out, whatever he thinks. The divorce is going through, and ChaCha is living with that man. French law prohibits you from disinheriting your own children, but I've worked it out so that dear Joe will get everything worthwhile. First and foremost, the proceeds from the sale of the apartment. In Paris *intra muros*, square meters are worth their dimensions in solid gold. As for my pension and savings, they'll go for the retirement residence. I know which one I want. It's just a matter of time until a place becomes available. I leave that in the hands of the Angel of Death--someone you can always count on. I'm referring to that sandstone building near the center of my provincial town here in France, the renovated eighteenth-century manor with the airy pillars and grounds that open on to the boulevard. The one they light up so delightfully at night; it looks like a fairy-tale, really, even if inside the princes and princesses—mainly princesses, of course--have decayed into humble witches, hunched over the fuming cauldrons of their memories.

STRAY

« We could go to my place for a nightcap. »

That's what this guy was saying, after we'd known each other for all of one hour at the Tadziki Bar on 30th Street. The surprising thing was that "OK" was out of my mouth, before the glaring, octagonal STOP sign that usually pops into my consciousness at this point could flaunt its white caps and bloody-Mary background.

I'd been simultaneously drawn to and wary of men since my divorce three years before. It wasn't that I didn't trust them exactly. It was my own judgment that was flawed, skewed, out-of-joint. If it hadn't been, I would never have been deceived in the first place, taken in by the flattery, the sob story, the lies, the appeals for patience and pity.

I had excuses: he was my first big crush, and I was only twenty. In fact, I fell for him to the point of the flouncy gown and all the paraphernalia of lifelong vows and the suburban- hotel wedding reception.

Then he started throwing the glassware against the wall and turning white-hot rages against me because of some inner demons whose names I didn't know. When the target became me and not the wall any more, I opted out.

My ex I could forgive, but myself? Did women come in dumber shades? And here I was now, a common pick-up in a bar, not drunk at all, saying "OK" with her eyes wide open. I had a good idea what nightcap meant, and I wasn't at all sure I was ready for that, even if this Pablo had gentle, smiling eyes and something like kindness in his voice. I'd been taken for a ride before, and this could be a whole lot worse.

I had a sudden flash of my own nude body splayed on a stained couch. There was a deep knife-wound to the belly and my head lay twisted to one side. My eyes were glazed over, and a martini glass—the nightcap—lay on a cheap felt carpet beneath my limp, dangling arm.

Don't ask what made me follow him. This is your chance, I heard in the back of my mind, and I went.

The building was your grungy, Bowery-style brick, complete with narrow staircase and smudgy, mustard walls; the occasional begonia wilting on a landing. Pablo's apartment had so-called two rooms, separated only by a sort of ridge in the floor that had once been a partition. There was a stained couch and the carpeting was made of cheap felt.

"Please don't mind the housekeeping," he said, as my gaze took in the book-lined walls, the kitchenette, the desk, the computer, more books. Pablo was kneeling in front of a low cupboard with bottles of various sizes and liquid levels. He had on frayed, cut-off jeans and a tight scarf on his head like the Projects kids, with one gold earring, your half-African-American-half-Hispanic dealer type. Short, dark, and beguiling.

He grinned at me: "How about a martini?" His accent was straight urban ghetto.

I clutched my bag and said, "Sure," then, "You've got a lot of books."

"Yep," he replied good-naturedly. "They're a fire-hazard. Hope no one comes to inspect. Plus the super doesn't allow animals in the building."

"Animals?"

"Meet Sassy." From a flat box on top of the radiator, just at window-sill level, he drew a sleepy, lanky, preteen cat, all pointy ears and elongated muzzle, eyes as green as traffic-lights in the pitch-black triangle of its impish, feline face.

"Got her from the shelter just in the nick. She had an ear infection, fleas, malnutrition. Mistreated probably. But I saved her. Now she's been vaccinated, vermifuged, and all she needs is to catch up her normal weight. An orphan—unwanted child of the welfare system!"

He held the young cat against his chest, and the creature stretched its sinewy forepaws upward, climbing his torso, and settled in the niche between neck and broad shoulder. Then it blinked its luminous eyes and purred.

"Sassy's just a beginning. See the books here? First year vet school. Fall term starts in a week. This is something I've always wanted to do. No more teaching Spanish to the ungrateful unwashed," he chuckled. "You like cats?" I heard a sudden worry note of mistrust in his voice.

"I love them," I said. "This one's a little Hollywood star. She's got on a real mink coat." I held out my hand to stroke Sassy's back, and she melted into Pablo's shoulder like black butter into toast. The purring became raucous.

I knew it would be all right. I'd have the martini, and maybe he'd take me home—another stray, after all—and then we'd meet again. And, really, this time it was going to be OK.

SUGAR DADDY

Five years after the fact, André discovered he was a father. The news had come in the form of a Polaroid snapshot: a wide-eyed little girl with very straight, very brown hair, pressing against a pair of adult legs in black, flared jeans. The picture didn't show Alicia's face, but he recognized the slender limbs, the way she held her feet, with the left one pointing inward ever so slightly. He used to think her stance was quaint, proof of a shy temperament. If she was retiring, she was also ferociously proud and secretive. But such a secret as this?

He'd studied the picture carefully. There was no denying it. She looked like him. He'd seen innumerable childhood pictures of himself at his parents' home in Arles, and something in the little girl's puzzled stare reminded him undeniably of himself at the same age. Beyond astonishment, his first emotion in front of the picture was anger. It crashed in bitter heaves inside his chest and made his diaphragm ache, as if he'd been running too fast and too much. He felt deceived and totally disarmed, defeated. Why hadn't she told him? Why had she waited? If it wasn't because she needed money, then why tell him at all? Did she expect him to feel paternal stirrings at this point in history, their history, his own?

And there was another question: why had Alicia simultaneously deprived his parents of their role as grandparents? Should he tell them? If he were to establish any sort of relationship with his daughter, then he would have to.

Non et merde, he would not. Neither establish nor tell. He would send money, even if Alicia hadn't asked for any. He'd make certain the child had an account in her own name, where he could make deposits, wired from France. But that would be all.

Alicia hadn't considered him worthy; she'd blanked him out of her life. Even now, and in spite of the overture the picture represented, she was asking nothing, at least not in plain language. It was wonder enough that she'd kept his child. He wasn't going to reappear with a teddy bear under his arm and a packet of lollipops.

Besides, at the time of the photograph, there'd been Hélène to think of. They'd met shortly after André had moved back to France and taken up his post again at the University of Aix-Marseille. She'd been in his department in Aix, *Lettres Modernes*, as a junior lecturer, and she'd asked him to direct her dissertation. Hélène was bird-frail and blond, unlike Alicia, who was regally tall, chestnut-haired, and walked as though she had the Harrap's Collegiate on her head.

About a year after she'd begun living with him, Hélène had fallen gravely, desperately ill. She had one of those cancers that violate the bodies of young people and send toxins pulsating through their lymph glands. They'd saved Hélène, thanks to burning remedies nearly as poisonous as the illness itself, and at the cost of her reproductive system. She would never have children. That, she said, was why she wouldn't marry him. One day, he'd find a woman who would give him a child. Anyway, how long did she have for this earth? she would add, cuddling into his warmth, imbibing his energy, begging tenderness and consolation.

He wasn't going to tell Hélène he already had a daughter: *Melody*. What sort of name was Melody? Something only an American mother would choose—out of a knitting catalogue, probably. Baby patterns. He had to smile at his dramatized contempt; Alicia was never one to do handcrafts of any kind.

Alicia, too, had been his student, the year he'd spent at Yale spreading the good word of twentieth century French literature. She'd been in the Master's program and had followed him around with a coterie of graduate students, all girls, who'd elected him their guru of the year: the handsome young Frenchman with the funny, incomplete nasals of Provence in his speech and the hazel eyes brimming with sunlight and poetry: Reverdy, Aragon, Eluard.

They all dreamed of sleeping with him, or so he thought. Every day, they'd join him after lunch for heavy little cups of piping-hot expresso, then wander the campus lawns, questioning him about the cafés of Paris, the lavender of Haute Provence, or maybe Marcel Proust. He imagined himself in a toga, Socrates of the Sisterhood, as he called his groupies, anointing the savage American breast with the dew of his knowledge.

Only for Alicia was the dew more physical. In his mind, she remained indissociable from the warm, genteel polish of the library, where they would meet in a far corner of the main reference room. Their hands first touched under the glow of a green-shaded reading lamp. The stacks rose behind her, and her dark hair shone against the reds and golds of venerable, leather-bound volumes.

Alicia began coming to his apartment for private tutorials. At occasional, anxious moments, André would imagine the consequences if she should suddenly, for reasons not yet established or fathomable, report him for…what? Seduction? Sexual harassment? That was such a widespread obsession among American women that it seemed an eventuality to be considered. Corrupting a minor could be eliminated; Alicia was of age. But no, she'd told him she loved him.

When he thought back on that year, André could never be certain she had actually pronounced those words. He thought that he hadn't either, but it went without saying that he felt at ease in her company. She was no gum-chewing, cheerleading ingenue. She'd read her classics and minored in philosophy. Alicia had class.

He hadn't understood when, nearing the end of the academic year, she'd stopped attending his lectures—a fact that didn't prevent her from passing the final with flying colors. Her telephone went unanswered, and when he asked the Sisterhood about her (as casually as he could), they muttered something about a sick parent, a return to Cincinnati. He went to the airport alone and boarded his return flight to Charles de Gaulle (with a transfer to Marseille-Marignane), while a kaleidoscope of Connecticut colors and odors continued to spin in his mind.

Progressively, they'd faded, replaced by the familiar, radiant light of Provence and the emanations of sun-baked thyme and fallen pine-needles. Only in the surrounding countryside did he occasionally find a village green enough to recall, in a modest way, the dramatic emerald of spring foliage on the New Haven campus. Never again did he feel that particular quality of the air that, like a damp wash-cloth, would lie against his skin, exalting the fragrance of grass. André wrote to Alicia, several times in fact, but he had only her college address. The letters were never returned nor were they ever answered.

Until the "Melody announcement letter"—ever so brief—and the photograph. And now, centuries—that is, nineteen years--later, he held another letter, this one without a photograph but written by Melody herself. He reread it for the fourth time:

Cher Père,

I'm capable of nothing more than the salutation in French—unfortunately, I didn't inherit my mother's gift for languages—but, since you are, indeed, my Père, I have been wanting to contact you. I must tell you that Mom is gone. She passed away six months ago from severe injuries sustained in a car crash.

(Alicia, dead? Had she ever really existed? Had she had a job, a career? A husband, perhaps? Lovers? Had she matured? Turned into a forty-something woman? Put on weight? Had her hair frosted to hide incipient gray? How can those who have never lived for us affront us by dying?)

Luckily, I'm not alone, but I think perhaps the time has come for us to meet. On the tenth of June, I'll be receiving my PhD. in psychology from Yale University, and I'd like to invite you to attend the ceremony. It is largely thanks to the money you've sent me over the years, that I've been able to afford my education.

I hope my letter won't come as too much of a shock. I hope also that we may, at long last, become acquainted, although I realize your life has gone on for many years without your American child, and that you may wish for it to continue that way—in which case, I'll understand.

Your daughter, Melody Wellington

Without a second's hesitation, he knew he would go. He even felt an odd agitation at the prospect, something between panic and exhilaration. It was indecent to rejoice at Alicia's death. At the same time, he knew he owed this event the opportunity to meet his daughter. At fifty-four now, he'd begun weeding the excess out of his life: intellectual ambition, the recognition of peers, even material success. Family had begun to count, and he had so little. He and Hélène had never broken off, but rather drifted apart. She'd been assigned to the university in Bordeaux, her native city, and they'd kept up a railroad relationship for several years, along with the pretense that he would request reassignment and join her. He had no real desire to leave Provence and put it off year after year. Now, they mainly exchanged letters, like old pen-pals, wondering sometimes what to write about.

He lacked no inspiration in answering Melody, however, and blackened page after page with explanations, longings, regrets—then threw the lot into the waste paper basket. He finally sent off a laconic but (he hoped) warm note, saying how pleased he would be to attend her graduation ceremony. He decided to come a month (at least) ahead of the date to spend a little more time in his past haunts, to (he had to admit to himself) have a chance to get to know her. He promptly requested a leave of absence from his own year-end obligations, for "imperative family reasons." The dean, assuming a dying parent, granted it.

She was pressing against the rope at arrivals in Newark, holding a computer-printed sign with his name on it. He'd half expected to see Alicia, reissued, but the young woman waiting for him was shorter, with straighter hair tamed by a winding strip of leather, and hazel eyes—his own, he saw that immediately—sharp and questioning, behind outdated (to a Frenchman) tortoise-shell rimmed glasses. All ideas of playing the self-composed intellectual, the prodigal yet sophisticated European father, the aloof but open-minded elder, melted in the light of that inquiring gaze. He found himself blushing furiously, stammering out of control, whatever English he still possessed gone haywire, even dropping his attaché case on her foot, which elicited a peal of laughter—perhaps nervous, too, but he wouldn't have wanted her to be otherwise.

"Follow me to the car," she said, recovering her composure. "I'm in the first parking lot, row ten." She smiled at him, not a constrained smile of circumstance, he was certain, but a friendly, forgiving (he knew he was reading that into it) smile of near, yes, near complicity. Had she gone down on her knees and said, "I adore and admire you, and I'm yours forever," he could not have fallen more suddenly, more thoroughly, or more poignantly in love. André was transpierced; the sensation was physically painful, like a stab-wound to the heart. He had never felt anything like it and wondered for the first time in his life if he oughtn't to believe in God.

Melody glanced in his direction as she drove. "I don't know what to call you," she said, with the spontaneous frankness he'd always appreciated in Americans.

" 'André' will be fine."

"What about 'Père'?" she said, almost mischievously, making it sound like "pair" as in "pair of socks."

"You choose then," he said, trying to sound lighthearted. " I'm not sure the particular label suits very well."

"If the shoe fits, wear it," she said, actually laughing now. It occurred to him she wasn't bitter, and that she was calmly mocking him. He'd dreamed many scenarios, foreseen a multitude of reactions, most of them negative—awkwardness, indifference, and even outright hostility--but humor had never crossed his mind. She was brilliant, this daughter of his, self-possessed and wise. He thrashed about in the ocean-waves of love, and still they swept his being, beating against him with all the force of their novelty.

"You'll be my guest this evening at dinner?" he ventured, fearing refusal like a shaky suitor.

"Tonight, you must rest," she answered. "Tomorrow will be time enough. We haven't spoken for twenty-four years. One more evening can hardly matter."

In fitful sleep, André dreamed of her. During his waking moments, he realized he'd had the *coup de foudre*, the stroke of lightning—ah, French was more poetic than English, with its matter-of-fact "love at first sight." "Thunderstruck" said it better. This wonderful child was his: his own blood coursed in her veins; his genes peopled her cells. No, no, he wasn't forgetting Alicia, apparent in the girl's easy grace and bearing, the rich chestnut of her hair, the curiosity that livened her features.

And only an American upbringing could have brought her that confident attitude of immediate trust.

Seated opposite him in a pricey restaurant near Broadway, her eyes raked his aging face. What did she see there? he wondered. Was their resemblance apparent to her, past the lines and furrows? He was still handsome for his age, distinguished (he thought), with only a hint of silver in his hair. Many women looked at him with interest, but although it gratified his vanity, André paid no attention. Life had lost much of its appeal in recent years. But now there would be Melody. Had she visited France? Did she know where his people came from? *Her* people, *nom de nom*! He wanted to ask her so many things, but first, *why*. Why had Alicia deserted him all those years ago without a a moment's hesitation, and what had she told their child?

A waiter appeared, boyish and effeminate; André endured the listing and contents of the day's specials—enough for five restaurants where he came from. "You choose for me," he told Melody, and, with a glint in her eye, she requested one dish for herself, another for "the gentleman." He felt a twinge of disappointment. Another time she would say, "for my father." He would tame her. His questions, on the other hand, burned in urgency. "Melody, what did your mother tell you about me? Did she marry? Do you have a step-father?"

"Mom never married. But she could have, any number of times. She was so smart, and she was a beautiful woman, still, at forty-seven." Her eyes widened; she was seeing something he could not.

"I'm so sorry," he said, feeling the inadequacy of it.

To his surprise, she burst into tears, then, calming herself, daubed at her cheeks with her napkin and looked straight at him again.

"I just…you see, I never understood why she dropped me like that." He could hear himself blundering. "She never told me she was expecting you."

"*She* dumped *you*?" Melody sounded incredulous. " That's not the version I heard."

"What did you hear?"

"Well, when I was little, she didn't tell me anything, of course, except a fairy-tale about this mysterious, faraway papa I had, who lived in a foreign land and couldn't come to visit."

"Did that satisfy you?"

"Oh, for a short time. She was actually pretty evasive, but when I was thirteen, she told me the whole story. I mean, how you'd two-timed on her with Linda."

"Linda?" André was flabbergasted, frozen with disbelief. "But I never even knew any Linda."

Melody looked at him hard. "Mom told me Linda was another girl in that group of students you used to go around with. Mom had believed you were in love with her, when all the time you were shagging this Linda person." In the face of André's horrified frown, Alicia paused. "Apparently Linda boasted about…about your prowess."

"And your mother believed her… I don't even remember a Linda. Melody, I swear to you by all that is sacred. If this Linda existed, she was good for one thing: a prize in fiction. She was a…a raving mythomaniac. Never, never did I have another American girlfriend."

"So Linda was taking her fantasies for reality?"

"Quite obviously."

"And my mother bought her innuendo at face value?"

"It would seem she did."

"Oh Lord, and that's why I missed out on having a father for twenty-four years?" She shook her head. "Mom was a fiercely loyal person but very, very independent. She might not have married you anyway… But still… "

"*Mélodie* (her name came out sheer French), it is all past. Do not hold anything against your mother. She wanted to do what she thought was best for you and for herself. "

"I've never doubted that."

"We can't rewrite the past, but we can set the record straight and begin a new chapter now for ourselves, you and me, daughter and… 'Père.'" He tried to smile as easily as Melody had, when she'd given him that name. In all his imaginings, the effect it would have on him had never crossed his mind. A phrase from her letter suddenly returned to him. "You wrote that you were not alone. You have a suitor? A beau, as the, uh, English goes?"

This elicited a wan, slightly absent smile; Melody's mind was elsewhere, wondering if she ought to, if, in fact, she could bear to deconstruct twelve years of misconception. Her birth father, as she thought of him, was a womanizer. That was a hard fact she'd simply had to live with. It was easier than thinking there had been an awful, life-determining mistake, and that twenty-four years of separation were twenty-four years of love lost. She wanted to push it from her consciousness, but she knew it would dog her now. With an effort, she brought herself back to the present. "Yes, I have a 'beau'. Oh, a very handsome one, very accomplished. In fact, we're planning on getting married, probably in the fall."

"What does he do?"

"Financial consultant. He has a Wall Street Office."

"Oh ho! A 'golden boy,' as we say in France? A financial wizard?"

"Well, you might say that. He's had a good measure of success."

"What is his name?"

"John."

Was there any first name more common? It revealed no clue, and André hesitated to ask the last name. He wanted to appear supportive, not prying. Melody might conclude that by asking the boy's last name, André was pressing at family background, religion, social status, ethnic origin, so many things that could be suggested but never proven. What did it matter? He'd find out soon enough. "John will be at the graduation ceremony, of course?"

"I'm afraid not," she said. "He'd have loved to, but there's a huge board meeting that very day that he can't possibly miss."

"I'll see him another time, then."

"Of course. I'll be sure you two are introduced before you fly back."

Already she was thinking of his departure, when he had only just arrived. She had wanted to meet him, and now she was satisfied. She had no particular intention of detaining him (not yet, anyway). So be it. He would win her confidence, inch by inch. Without weighing on her, he would make every minute of his stay count.

"Have you got a snapshot of John?" he asked.

"Oh, not on me. Sorry. But you'll meet, don't worry. "

ණ

André left New York for New Haven, where he took a room near enough the campus to meet Melody easily for lunch—frequently, if not daily. The cups of expresso such as he'd enjoyed years ago with Alicia were now downed in the company of her daughter—his daughter, too, he thought, feeling the swell of pride that continued to astonish and ravish him. He showed her family snapshots, the French grandparents she hadn't known, and pictures of Aix-en-Provence: the fountain of the Four Dolphins, the Place d'Albertas, the Cathédrale Saint-Sauveur, the Bibliothèque Méjane, the Cours Mirabeau with its plane-tree shaded cafés. "When you come…," he would repeat, while Melody would tilt her head and smile non-committally.

He rather enjoyed imagining the financial whiz she'd chosen: business suit (only out of obligation), brisk walk, attaché case under one arm, electronic agenda—an honest, energetic young man who would provide a secure, stable life for her. He would commute to the heart of the city, while Melody would be free to hang out her psychologist's shingle. Oh, he would have preferred an academic like himself for Melody, one of those passionate, young American scholars devouring the fabulous libraries the country put at everyone's disposal, but her choice was sacred. André even found himself entertaining the idea of grandchildren in his fantasies: two or three chestnut-haired (like their mother) tykes who would summer in Provence, become rapidly bilingual, and climb onto Grandpère's lap, demanding love and stories. Surely, there would be at least one grandchild. André would, after all these years, have a youngster to lavish his (newfound) affection on.

His phone rang. John was coming up from the city, Melody announced, and would André like to meet him? An appointment was made for dinner.

ঌ

André watched the couple enter, navigate the noisy crowd of diners. His first thought was, But where is her young man? At Melody's side was someone André could only describe as "a mature gentleman," about his own age, probably five or six years older—seriously encroaching on sixty, in other words—with thinning salt-and-pepper hair and a very slight stoop to his shoulders. The fellow's father, he told himself, feeling, nonetheless, a sudden spark of panic ignite.

Melody spotted him and waved, tugging slightly on the gray-haired man's sleeve. Her smile was broad as she introduced him: "Père, this is John. John, my long-lost father, André." André willed himself to rise, to shake the hand that was offered, to calm his heart-beat gone wild. How could she, how could she, how could she... ?

❧

As he tossed in bed that night, he convinced himself that she couldn't. Not love, the fellow, not possibly. It was obvious she had lacked a father. That was the long and short of it. No need to read Doctor Freud for that to strike loud and clear. She wanted the assurance of material comfort, the advice and approval of an older man—but love him, she could not. And he, the pervert, taking advantage of a naïve, idealistic young woman! Of course, it was hard to blame him. Melody of the winning ways, the sparkling eyes. Why should he resist a banquet offered? I have arrived in the nick, André thought, sweating profusely in his over-heated hotel room. I will save her from the clutches of this--this pedophile!

André realized he was treading on eggshells. He would have to unravel his subtlest French diplomacy in order for Melody to discover, as if on her own, that this John could never be a husband for her. And to think he had gone so far as to imagine grandchildren. If the marriage went through and children there were (how could that even be thinkable?), they would have no father but two grandfathers. *Ugh*, the very thought disgusted him. Never would he share any grandchild of his with a graying *vieux beau, un papa-gâteau*—a sugar daddy! He resolved to speak to her in the morning. If he didn't talk to her immediately, his life would be unending torture.

Melody asked to put their meeting off until later. She was having lunch with John, she said, but she'd be free later, when he returned to New York. On the phone she sounded happy, carefree. "What's the big rush?" she asked, as if slightly amused. "We only just saw each other last night." André wondered if she sensed what was bothering him. She must; her degree was in psychology, after all. So why hadn't she warned him? Well, he had asked no questions. He hadn't wanted to.

ஒ

However hard he tried, André could not keep his voice even. He felt the blood rush to his face, imagined himself ridiculously congested and purple, and only blushed more violently. He leaned across the table. "My dear child," he said, "*ma Mélodie*"… Surely you aren't really planning to marry this *monsieur*…Watkins…John. Do tell me I have misunderstood. He is an old friend of your mother's who has known and loved you since childhood—in a fatherly sort of way, of course. But marriage, no… I realize you needed support—the kind I ought to have given you, and that circumstances prevented me from providing. You know now how I regret that, Melody. This being said, I am here now, and I want to give you the advice of a man who is older than you and loves you as a true father. Do not throw your youth and beauty away on someone so…"

"So old?" She laughed. "I suspected that was it. Don't worry, Père! John is wonderfully fit. Do you know, he goes sailing every weekend? If I'm not there, he goes alone or with another banker friend of his. His boat's at a New Jersey yacht club. And as far as working out is concerned…

"His yacht," André interrupted. " I see. Melody, I can understand you would be attracted to him for his money—your childhood was a long period of deprivation--but please, reflect on this."

"It's not that, Père. John is…well, he's just a wonderful person." Her eyes crinkled at the corners, "and a wonderful lover."

André felt nausea wash over him. He pushed away the absurdly overloaded plate he'd been served. The heavy, pervasive smell of frying sickened him. Why did these American restaurants always have to reek of deep fat?

Melody was studying his face. She added softly, "Even if he were to lose his fortune, I would still marry him." Her tone was gently firm.

André felt like a drowning man, and all he could thrash out at were the buoys of cliché: *I'm warning you for your own good; all I want is for you to be happy.* Beneath the hackneyed phrases, he could hear his own disappointment and, yes, jealousy. Don't leave me for this other "father." I'm here now. A young man, yes, I can accept, a father for my grandchildren, but not someone who cannot be anything more to you than I am. A lover? Preposterous. You have your life ahead of you. And he? How many years to live? Do you want to spend the bloom of your prime caring for a senile invalid? He brought his breathing under control and managed a smile.

Melody pressed his hand.

André made his way to the station, where he boarded the New York train. He would check the yellow pages for firearms, then get a taxi directly to the shop. They hardly asked any questions here, he knew that. Everyone said it was absurdly easy. He had his maroon passport with him (*Communauté européenne, République française*). They'd want to know if he had a police record, a history of mental illness. He was a foreigner--there might be a perfunctory check—perhaps a couple days' wait. No matter. He imagined how the thing would feel in the palm of his hand: heavy, metallic, cold and hard.

Melody. The name that at first had sounded silly to his ears sang to him like the theme from a symphony. It was exactly what she had brought to his life: music. I could have danced through life, he thought. If only, when she was five years old, I had run to her and seized her in my arms. I never once considered what it might feel like to a child--not knowing who her father was.

Lack of imagination carried a high price. Why should anyone other than himself be held accountable? The lethal chic of the small revolver weighed against his thigh. The buildings of Wall Street oppressed him, casting long afternoon shadows on the sidewalk. Time for offices to empty out. André watched as businessmen and -women, most of them youthful and preoccupied, hurried past: time to catch a subway train, time to race home to upper Manhattan, to Queens, to the suburbs of New Jersey or Staten Island or Brooklyn. He caught sight of a graying head, shoulders bent slightly forward. André's hand tightened on his weapon. He saw the man closer up: he wore thick, plastic-rimmed glasses and looked nothing at all like John Watkins. And even so—the gun was empty of ammunition.

No guts, André told himself. Not interested in my child when it was still time, not interested enough in her mother to track her down when first she'd fled, not interested enough in Hélène to insist on making a life with her, not even truly interested in my research and my students. André walked to the tip of Battery Park. He felt for the bullet in his left pocket.

He heard the wail of an ambulance driving off, or was it a police car? Near the water's edge, a small crowd huddled, discussing something that must have occurred moments before. He overheard snatches of conversation:

"... put an end to it all."

"Poor, pathetic fellow."

"Some people have no courage."

"Don't say that; you don't know what he was feeling."

"Suicide's the easy way out."

André turned on his heel, seeking the subway entrance.

He sent Melody a generous gift of money in honor of her doctorate. He was so sorry he couldn't be there after all, he'd written. He'd been called back to France by his publisher, the one bringing out his study in September on the playwright, Bernard-Marie Koltès. He was needed urgently for several promotional appearances in June. Readers have to be tantalized in advance. A Koltès play was on at the Théâtre Montparnasse, and an unexpected opportunity to participate in a panel of drama critics and university experts had arisen. André's study of Koltès was real; the panel was a pure fabrication.

Hélène wrote to him about a possible opening in the French Literature department in Bordeaux for the following academic year. They spent the summer hunting for an apartment to share. He didn't know if the post could be his but chose to act as if it was going to be. Another year spent commuting, and then they would really be together. André decided to put his parents' provençal house up for sale. He wasn't sure there would be anyone he'd leave it to.

Just as the intitial buzz over his Koltès book was subsiding, André received a letter from Melody. He opened the envelope and drew out a snapshot of her in cap and gown—a magnificent, black gown such as doctoral students wore, with a crimson velvet hood and stripes on the flowing sleeves. She appeared to be on a podium, shaking the hand of an academic—certainly the dean. The envelope remained stiff, and André realized there was a second snapshot in it. There was Melody again, this time in a sweatshirt with wind whipping her straight hair. She was leaning against a tan, broad-shouldered young man. There was a vast expanse of blue sky behind them. They seemed to be in the country, or perhaps at the beach, and their pose spoke of holidays and easy intimacy.

André unfolded the letter. Like an earlier one, it began:

Cher Père,

Here are two little souvenirs for you: one shows your daughter receiving her sheepskin. The other is of Dave and me at Sandy Hook. Dave is my new boyfriend. We've barely been together a month now, but I can't tell you how happy I am…

Fatima Gives Birth

And the fruits shall surpass the flowers' promise.
Malherbe

Fatima's hair was obsidian-black and tumbled in secret waves beneath a coarse linen headscarf. The cloth was ruddy, splashed with dark blue flowers. An unruly tendril had escaped from the left fold and clung to her temple. When Elizabeth saw her for the first time, Fatima was four months pregnant. Her robust, country-girl arms rested on her belly, already rounding with the promise of fruit.

"Liz, let me introduce your student," bustled Fran, head of Literacy. "She's from Algeria. Refugee Welcome Program. She doesn't know how to read at all."

Is she announcing this with satisfaction? Or do I just hear matter-of-factness?

"Good morning, Meessiz." Fatima gazed at Elizabeth with dark-eyed serenity.

The "r" in her greeting cooed gently. Her smile was circumstantial, polite, a bit indifferent.

"I'm Elizabeth." She held out a hand, while Fatima rose heavily from the straight-backed public library chair to extend her own. The long name met with a blank. "*Liz* will be fine." She told Fatima how happy she was to be working with her, and at last some inner dawn lit up the young woman's features.

"It's her husband who wants her to learn," said Fran. "He came to the office with her last week. They've been in this country about six months. He wants her to have some English to help her in her everyday life. She speaks it a wee bit; that's all."

Illiterate, barely speaking the language... a truly impoverished student. Fatima would be Elizabeth's challenge. She'd have to rise to new, inventive teaching heights. Years dealing with college students hadn't prepared her for the ABCs, but she'd worked with several refugees now, and they had progressed. Elizabeth brushed a graying lock from her eyes and frowned slightly, reflecting.

Fatima's husband must be a good man, she was thinking Weren't people accustomed to taking Arabs for macho partners who willingly abandoned their wives to ignorance in order to keep the upper hand? Here was one who wanted his wife to learn. Honorable of the fellow. Another thought immediately flitted ahead of the previous one. He probably wanted Fatima to learn to read in order to send her out to work. Since she had no professional qualifications, she'd end up a cleaning woman, having conquered the Alpine peaks of language in order to push a vacuum cleaner around the well-appointed living rooms of wealthier than she.

Well, and so what? Fatima and I will prove to him that a woman who can read can also accomplish miracles. Reading will just be the beginning. Later, we'll talk about education, training, degrees...

Hopeful thoughts jostled for a moment in Elizabeth's mind. Fran left with a cheerful nod, and then it was time to take their places at the corner table near the Mystery Fiction section and begin the lesson. Fatima sat down again and pulled from a large, otherwise empty plastic bag a new spiral notebook and a blue Bic pen.

Will she know how to hold a pen?

Seated opposite her teacher, ready to tackle the lined page, Fatima appeared, in fact, to have been born with pen in hand.

"So, is it true? You don't know how to read? You've never written?"

"She say that to you, Messiz? No, not so. I write Arabic."

Once more, Elizabeth felt annoyance at Fran rising from diaphragm to throat, touching her cheeks with the dark pink of embarrassment: that word of Fran's—*literacy*.

When will she come to agree that someone who doesn't know English but can read and write his own language is not an illiterate? That the very term of "literacy" is scornful, offensive, and ethnocentric? You don't speak English? You haven't mastered the Latin alphabet? Ah, poor thing; you are illiterate, even if you have in the depths of your pocket a PhD. from the University of Saint-Petersburg. No, it is we who purvey culture and civilization. Come to our Literacy lessons, and the gospel of language shall be revealed unto you.

Elizabeth had argued unsuccessfully for their volunteer service unit to be known as "ESL": English as a Second Language.

"You did go to school, then?" she asked Fatima.

"I go three years. Five years old to eight years old. I know the letters in Arabic."

Here was no doctoral candidate. Elizabeth would still have her hands full, but someone who has learned an alphabet, albeit one that begins on the right of the page, can certainly learn another. The job wouldn't be so daunting after all. She'd begin by writing out the twenty-six letters for Fatima. *Horror of horrors!* There would be printed capitals first, then printed lower-case letters, not to mention scripted caps and small letters. Too many summits to scale before they'd have their tools in hand. Elizabeth bowed her head a moment, pressing fingertips to temples.

This was it! She'd limit their first foray into the alphabet to the vowels and consonants of Fatima's name. When, at the end of an hour, the girl had learned to put the *F* at the beginning, the *T* in the middle, and surround the *M* with its squiggly comrades, Elizabeth hugged her pupil enthusiastically. She gratified Elizabeth a second time with the light of her smile, said "Good-bye, Meessiz," (no "thank you" was audible), and, tightening the rough material of her mantilla around her head and shoulders, walked swiftly through the wide main doors of the library.

The following week, she had forgotten everything.

On the evening after the lesson, Elizabeth pulled from her shelves a ragged old handbook, refugee from some used book sale, and which had hung out unemployed in her library for long, dusty years. She ran the side of her hand over the dull red cover. It smelled of time and disuse. The text was entitled *First Book of Classical Arabic, sixth edition*, and had been published in Algiers. Never before had it occurred to her to look at it closely, but suddenly the explanations of its author, a certain Kamel Jijelli, professor at the University of Constantine, stood out as urgently compelling. By the second page, she was bewildered, by the third discouraged, and by the fourth, faced with "intitial, medial, and final interdentals," she threw in her towel. If she could not progress beyond the fourth page of the Arabic textbook, how could Fatima, with her three meager years at elementary school, seize in a few weeks the keys to the English language?

Filled with poignant empathy, she dreamed up lessons on the Latin alphabet that aimed at mixing the fantasy of comic strips with the charm of children's books. To illustrate "o" she drew a boat, for the long "a" sound a bundle of hay. Fatima never smiled at these little finds which only mystified her.

Elizabeth gave her writing exercises for the following lesson, and the Algerian girl brought them back carefully executed, the letters in rows like good little soldiers: the round "a's" with their pigtails on the side, the dancing "i's" capped with their dots, the triple hills of handwritten "m" huddled together for warmth. When the teacher clapped with joy to congratulate the pupil, she confessed that it was Jafar, her husband, who had written them.

"Why," Elizabeth asked her, "did you stop school at the age of eight?"

Fatima shrugged. "That's how it was for girls. At nine, you had to walk more far to another school, three kilometers. Our mamas didn't want. OK for boys; they went, but a girl stays at home."

"And you agreed to that? You weren't disappointed?"

"No. Why? A girl, she cooks. You don't need to know read and write."

Elizabeth shook her head, removed her glasses slowly and placed them on the table. So, Fatima was not her ally. She bore the lessons passively just as she must have borne her household obligations. Why? In order to get out in the afternoon? To please her husband? To obey him? She didn't know, then, that reading is an immense privilege?

It will be my crusade. I shall convince her of this.

"Fatima, if you learn how to read, think of all it will bring you."

"What?"

The girl was sincerely perplexed. Her dark eyebrows lifted like two question marks.

"Well, you can discover the world, a whole universe of things you don't know. Those things are in books."

Fatima looked at her curiously. *What's the use of learning about our vast world when you're happy at home?*

The usefulness of reading was so obvious that Elizabeth found herself fumbling (*oh, shame!*) for arguments. "You can…" she hesitated… "read stories to your child. You'll be able to help him later with his homework. You won't be lost in town when you go on errands."

"I'm not lost," she replied flatly, and, indeed, Elizabeth easily imagined her in the aisles of the supermarket, her floral scarf carefully knotted, pushing a heavy-laden cart. No need to master reading and writing to choose your zucchini, your onions, your tomatoes. Every can and box bears a picture. As for the baby, she would tell it stories; she would sing. She had never seen a book herself during her early childhood; how could she miss something she'd never known?

"Fatima, listen!" She just had to try again. "I know a book just looks to you like a lot of paper between closed doors, a sort of closet you can't enter. And if you could, you don't know why you should. But, believe me, if only you take that first step, you'll find such extraordinary things in it. You'll find beautiful words, words that surprise or excite you or comfort you, that tell you about who you *are*."

"About *me*? How?" Her frown was slightly suspicious.

"You'll read stories about people, and when we learn about other people, we find out all sort of things about ourselves. We're all human beings, after all, and writers explain our own hearts to us."

"Ah," she acquiesced, hoping to put an end to the odd tirade, gazing with near-pitying indulgence at her teacher. *How bizarre this woman is!*

Since Fatima could never recall her cleverly-drawn letters, Elizabeth quit the alphabetic approach. She wrote simple stories about the young woman's life, using short, easy words. *The baby is coming. It's here. Is it a boy? Is it a girl? Fatima is the mommy. She is happy.* Fatima applied herself, learned by heart, but the same words elsewhere, in other contexts, rang no bells.

Elizabeth tested her again on the subject of her husband. He wanted a boy, surely.

"No, he'll be glad if girl."

There were no two ways about it; this was a modern man, and stereotypes die hard. Fatima was the backward one, with her head in the ragout pot, her hands in her apron pockets. Perhaps, Elizabeth thought, she could catch her interest with exciting narratives, stories whose outcome the girl would be impatient to discover. She remembered the short stories you find in women's magazines. Later she would let herself dream of bringing romance novels and even classics: *Of Mice and Men. Pride and Prejudice. Jane Eyre.* She didn't want to be another Fran, but of course she couldn't teach this girl the literature of her own culture. Fatima was going to live in an English-speaking country, after all.

Our writers will be hers.

In the meantime, Elizabeth took to their library corner a bunch of those catalogues that slip regularly through mail slots, so that her student could practice by filling out virtual order forms. Still, the Algerian girl remained impassive: her apartment was already "nice furnished," she said, and Western clothes left her indifferent, disapproving even. Still, she dutifully filled in the blanks of an order sheet and glanced with amused tenderness at a brochure of baby equipment.

Fran greeted Elizabeth at the next lesson, breathless and hot-cheeked. "I tried to call you at home, but you must have been on your way already. I wanted to tell you not to come today. Fatima's in the hospital."

"In the hospital? The baby? But it's too early, isn't it?"

"Exactly. She almost miscarried. Her husband called. He was very upset."

They weren't to see Fatima again during her pregnancy. She had to stay in bed, hooked like a wretched, freshly caught fish to a long IV, whose needle wounded the soft interior of her arm, violet from the bursting of fragile blood vessels. Elizabeth knew this for speaking regularly on the phone with Jafar. She would call for news of Fatima and then would write to her each week: short messages with simple words, the letters carefully printed. Sometimes she would send a postcard of their small Connecticut town showing places familiar to the girl: the square with its lush lawn and the white Congregational church, the baseball stadium, the village hall with its mock-Tudor windows. At other times, she would send a few words of encouragement on lavender notepaper with flower motifs. This was undoubtedly the first correspondence Fatima had ever received.

Elizabeth didn't visit her. She knew that the young woman's mother and two of her sisters, worried, had come from the city where they were housed to keep vigil by her bedside.

Later, she learned that Fatima's labor had been induced to avoid complications. She had suffered a great deal, and the child, a little girl they named Nadia, had almost died. But now both were out of danger, and Fatima, so Jafar said, had been allowed to come home.

Some days afterward, Elizabeth found in her mailbox a square, formal-looking envelope, addressed in an unknown hand. Jafar, she guessed. Inside another hand had held the pen, a less practiced although careful one. *The baby is here*, said the note. *Fatima is happy. See you soon. Thank you.* There were no mistakes. She had signed like a good schoolgirl, just as she had on the day of her first lesson.

Armed with a bouquet of pink roses, Elizabeth knocked at Jafar and Fatima's door. A mature woman, her face and upper body swathed in a voluminous black shawl, invited her in and led her to Fatima, half-supine on a sofa with her little girl pressed to her chest.

"Meessiz Leez, this is Nadia!" Fatima's smile was radiant, as she held out the child.

Elizabeth admired the baby's peachlike roundness, the golden down on her tiny arms, her chocolate-bean eyes.

"How pretty she is! I could eat her up!"

Elizabeth's gaze traveled from the infant to the coffee table, where pieces of fruit, pastel-colored cubes of Turkish delight, and more birth announcements, in what appeared to be Fatima's new handwriting, were scattered helter-skelter. Her eyes questioned the young mother.

"For our American friends. I prepared all. We didn't think we'd have her, our Nadia. We are so happy." She beamed at her teacher, then again at her little daughter. "Lots to do. We busy, right, Nadia?"

What Elizabeth heard was, *No more lessons for now, please!*

But she'd be back. The next time, she'd bring a children's book, one of the cloth ones that babies can touch and handle.

There would be Mother Goose next. And one day, she'd give the child fairy tales.

Nadia, you'll read them with your mother. Later, you'll tell her the marvelous stories you're learning at school. You'll sit by her and help her to read them along with you. And then, when you've grown up to a big girl, you'll be her best teacher. You'll tell her about the wonderful writers you've studied: Walter Scott and Scott Fitzgerald, O. Henry and Katherine Mansfield. Jane Austen and the Brontë sisters. Nadia, you'll tell her, won't you? About Jane Eyre…?

The Strength of the Armed Forces

La discipline fait la force des armées.
(Discipline is the strength of the armed forces.):
French saying

Margo wasn't born a disciplinarian. That's why she swore she would never, no never, teach in high school. Famous last words, as they say. That was before she met her French husband and, necessity being the mother of the work force, signed her soul away to the French Ministry of Education to teach English in a...well, let's not say high school; *lycée* sounds so cultured.

French *lycéens* have the reputation (deserved or not) of being well-behaved. And, indeed, they can be, if you possess the delicate French knack of the put-down. Send a Gallic smart-aleck a cutting remark or two in the teeth that will humiliate him in front of his thirty-three or so cohorts, and your peace and quiet are guaranteed for the remainder of the school year.

And if you haven't got the knack? What if you're a gentle New Englander, a pure pacifist at heart, with an ever-so-literary degree in French from a genteel, ivy-covered women's institution? Well, there you are, the Christian tossed to the lions, and all you can fall back on is your exotic (you hope) American charm to tame them.

Margo had always believed that ought to suffice, and, as a matter of fact, it most often did. But there will always be the hard nuts to crack, and Joël was one of those. He landed in her eleventh grade (*Classe de Première L,* for « *Littéraire* ») English class one morning in September at nine o'clock.

« 'ello! » he called, entering jauntily.

« Hello, » she smiled back.

She should have known better. She'd had enough experience to know that the French student, given a centimeter, will help himself to a kilometer. But there she was, Ms. Gullible from Massachusetts, still unable to get it right.

She described the scene to one of her French colleagues. « *I* would have sent him out and had him re-enter with a proper *Bonjour Madame*, » the woman frowned.

Some people never learn.

From that day on, Joël was the thorn that scratched her tender flesh. If there was an opportunity to do some clowning, he seized it. His incredible savvy told him just when her uttermost limit was about to be attained. She tried pop psychology: he just needs to be the center of attention, she told herself, and if I give him enough, he will feel rewarded and calm down. It was not attention Joël needed, but a swift kick somewhere. Nonetheless she remained patient. Too patient.

When he came out with some silly, non-à-propos remark, just to be sure everyone was noticing him, she would deflect it with humor (so she thought). Joël would gloat and consider that he had toted up another point on the class popularity score-board.

The hours with *Première L* went by far more slowly than those with Margo's other classes, and everyone seemed to get ready for the bell fifteen minutes too early. They began their recreation-time chats in her class, and the more Joël triumphed, the less hold she had on everyone else.

Thus, eleventh grade passed by for the *Classe de Première L*, and Joël, at the end of the year, had a passing grade in only one subject: English. This was not only because Margo was such a good-sport-soft-touch teacher, but because Joël was actually competent enough to scrape up a ten out of twenty average. Only occasionally did he stoop to doing assignments, but he absorbed the grammar by osmosis. Wasn't *that* a pity!

The class board of teachers met and agreed that Joël ought to repeat the eleventh grade. The French national system has decreed that the repetition of eleventh grade cannot be imposed. It can be a suggestion, never a commandment. But what teenager will voluntarily leave his friends, his classmates (and, in Joël's case, his audience) and stay back « for his own good »?

So, there was Joël, a grinning senior, in Margo's twelfth grade Advanced English class (supposedly reserved for the highly motivated). His triumphant smile did not last long, however. Joël had soured over the summer. The cheerful class clown had deteriorated into the scowling class rebel. Advanced English (*Anglais Renforcé*) meant studying real works by real authors, and Joël's gift for grammar would not get him by any longer. He was behind in every subject, out of his depth.

He went on strike: no book, no pen and paper, never any reading done. Stalwartly, Margo expelled him from class. He would return, Martyred and Oppressed. He took up steady conversation with his neighbor of the day, and, with thirty-five young people filling the room, there was no way to isolate him. He could divert the most studious, the most serious-minded. No classmate ever dared tell *Joël* to « shut up and listen! »

He excelled in his role of martyr. Whatever punishment Margo meted out to him, he would turn to his advantage. When he arrived late, she would send him downstairs to the office of the *surveillants*, the young people, university students, usually, in charge of attendance at French schools. They would accompany him to study hall and see that he got some busy work to do.

« But yesterday, » Joel protested, « you accepted Nancy. *She* was late. »

« Nancy is not usually late. She does her homework. She had a good excuse, and she's polite. Besides, *I*'m the one who decides who enters this class and who doesn't. »

« You see? » he called the thirty-four others to witness with a scornful shrug of his sweat-shirted shoulders (« Harvard's—*sic*-- University »). It was obvious that the American tyrant had it in for him.

School invariably gave Joël a headache, and the best place to ask for permission to the infirmary was English, especially twenty minutes before the last bell of the day.

« Stick it out, will you, Joël? » Margo would ask, and he would put on his rueful, long-suffering air and roll his eyes with a meaningful look in her direction that his neighbors couldn't miss. He was the victim, not she, of course. *She* was a nasty, unfair teacher, taking out her existential difficulties on an innocent, teenage boy. The nasty teacher broke out in a rash.

When Margo saw that she was becoming literally allergic to Joël, she knew the time for decisive action had come. His history teacher was sweating it out in very much the same way (Madame Dupassé was not from Massachusetts, but she could have been). Together, they sought out the aid of the head teacher, the philosophy teacher, before whose wrath the class trembled (Joël usually passed up the chance to go to philosophy).

The three teachers summoned Joël and his mother (no father on the scene). The tone was solemn, the setting impressive. Their school was situated in the renovated building of a seventeenth century edifice. The parlor reserved for parent-teacher conferences had a vaulted ceiling worthy of the Benedictine abbey it formerly was: a place for admonishment, not necessarily absolution.

Joël's mother was intimidated. No, she didn't know he never did his work. No, she didn't know he was failing his *Classe Terminale* (although this may sound like an illness, it is actually the last year of high school, the all-important year preceding the national examination, « *Le Bac* »).

« You may think you're the class entertainer, » Monsieur Dubanqué told him in his booming voice, « but actually, you're the laughing-stock of your classmates. They don't respect you, and that's why they let you continue to divert them at your own expense. It saddens me to see a young man so despised, » he added, with a flair for the dramatic and just a tinge of hypocrisy. « *They* know you'll never pass your *Bac*! »

Why hadn't Margo thought of saying that? She had to face it; a boot camp sergeant, she would never be.

Joël hung his head. He made resolutions. Monsieur Dubanqué made threats. Joël turned over a new leaf, if not a chapter.

His teachers sincerely hoped he would surprise them, but he did indeed fail his national exam at the end of the year and enrolled to repeat his *Classe Terminale.* Margo sighed on seeing that one of her co-English teachers had drawn his number for *her* class!

Three months before the examination, Joël gave it all up for good. He got a job at the frozen food store and then signed up for, of all things, the army.

No hard feelings, Joël, Margo thought. In her mind, she wished him well. In a way, hadn't he been her teacher too, letting her in on a secret or two about human nature and confronting her with some lackings of her own? Moreover, it was clear that somewhere, deep inside, Joël recognized his need for some *real* « dee-see-pleen, » French or otherwise.

FULBRIGHT SCHOLAR

Minneapolis

The acceptance letter for Claire's study grant was followed in short order by two congratulatory messages, one each from her Congressmen, Republican and Democratic. She'd "proven her worth," they'd said. All Claire knew was that at the end of the summer, she would take off for Paris, a city she'd fantasized about for so long, she'd begun to fear it actually might not measure up. Her imagination had been nourished for over a year now by the descriptions and narrations (snapshots to illustrate) of her French boyfriend, Philippe. Boulevards, sidewalk cafés, a jumble of shops, the classy and the alternative, ran in all directions through her mind. Geraniums tumbled out of wrought-iron window boxes, while sleek women in five-inch heels whisked by on the sidewalks below.

Philippe would be back there by the time she arrived, and they planned to take a flat together. Claire liked the word "flat," which sounded European, even if it brought to mind the words "cold-water" or "gas on every floor." Those came from reading all those early twentieth-century French novels. She projected herself into pages by Colette and Queneau, even if she knew Paris was as modern as it was antique.

Claire added the "i" to her name (the plain English spelling her parents had chosen was "Clare") and filled out advance forms for the University of Paris I. As for Philippe, he would be reading law at Paris-Dauphine and one day succeed his father in his notarial office. Philippe's parents had money, very old money, and an apartment opposite the Jardin du Luxembourg that would equal in surface the three stories of her own family house laid side to side. Philippe's home was no "flat," she thought, but the Parisian equivalent of a great, top-floor baseball diamond.

Instead of reading for her Master's, Claire spent much of the summer preparing her wardrobe. Even if Philippe assured her that jeans and a sweater were the international student uniform, she purchased a vaporous, low-waisted affair that made her feel she'd stepped into "*les années folles*," and a black, sharply tailored pants suit. In that, she was confident she'd strike a left-bank-intellectual note. Her winter clothes would be strictly Parisian. How much could you fit into the one suitcase airline companies allowed?

Books were heavy, and there were a number of those she had to pack, along with the reams of notes she'd already taken on her research project: "Sacred Prostitution in Antiquity." The BN, or Bibliothèque Nationale de France, housed documents she absolutely had to (that was the justification for her grant) consult, if she were to make progress in her subject.

Claire meant to concentrate on the Mesopotamian goddess, Ishtar (*"Princess of princesses, Goddess of goddesses, queen of all peoples, leader of humanity [...]goddess of men, god of women..."*). In one of her hymns, Ishtar declared herself "the compassionate prostitute." She was the female *eros* incarnate, mistress of life and death and of *hieros gamos*, the mystical union between sovereign and vestal. Claire's thesis involved demonstrating the symbolic power of The Sacred Prostitute. The words burbled in her throat like mouthwash. She could see herself (replete with black pants-suit chic) waving a graceful left hand in the air, her right touching the wrist of Philippe's mother or father or brother, while she ever-so-knowledgeably explained those notions to her captivated listener.

The day she received her B.A. degree with a double major in history and anthropology, Philippe presented her with a diamond ring that brought to mind the crystal doorknobs at her grandparents' house. She already had one passport to travel on; this bright-cold stone was a passport to the respectability Philippe's family was likely to require.

Chisinau

Stela's classmate, Vita, had brought her the ad—one of those little classifieds that occasionally appeared in the final pages of *Vremya.* She'd handed it to her, ringed in red ink, as they sauntered away from the high school after the last afternoon bell.

Paris restaurant seeks waitresses. No experience necessary. Immigration formalities simplified. To apply, call.........

"You're nuts," Stela told her. "Don't you know that's a white slavery trap?"

Government posters warned young women to flee such appeals like the plague. Behind the deceptive words lay networks of evil, scheming mafiosi, who bought and sold teenagers like chattel.

"You go and see those people, and you fall through a trapdoor, and that's it. You're drugged, gagged, and bound, and delivered to a brothel somewhere in southern Italy. Then they rape you and beat you to a pulp if you protest. Vita, they *do*!"

Vita was shaking her head. "Not this time, Stela," she assured.

"How do you know?" Stela narrowed her eyes. Vita's, blue as the Virgin's robe, were particularly round and guileless.

"Because I've called the number, and I've already *met* these people. I mean, their representatives in Chisinau. They're legitimate! It's a real restaurant, and they really need personnel. French girls won't work for peanuts like Moldavians will; it's a known fact. Stela, this is the chance of a lifetime."

"If it's such a chance, why aren't you going?" Stela tossed her blond hair.

"I *am* going! But they need another person, and that's why I'm showing you this. Of course, if you're not interested…"

"No, wait; of course I'm interested."

Vita had been looking pointedly at their classmate Ana, several steps ahead. Stela could never bear it, if Vita gave her dream away to someone else. Since she'd been little and had come across a book on French painting (Toulouse-Lautrec, Renoir) at the library, Stela had dreamed of Paris. Well, of

France, but Paris was France, as far as she knew. They had everything there, everything that could make you happy: majestic buildings, luxurious parks, the latest clothes, unheard-of foods and inebriating wines; swanky nightclubs, expensive cars, sexy make-up, work for anyone who needed it, money for anyone who wanted it. There were none of those things in her parents' village, or even in town, where her high school was. Her heart was already racing. "Should I call the number?"

"Just leave it to me," Vita told her. "I know the guy in charge. He's really nice. I'll tell him you're OK for an interview. I'll arrange for it for after school tomorrow. I mean, unless you change your mind. Don't feel you have to or anything. They're bound to find someone."

"Tomorrow's fine."

Stela could see the Eiffel Tower. Then she was shopping in the arcades of la rue de Rivoli. A handsome French boy was pouring her a glass of wine in a sidewalk café. He smiled as he bent toward her.

"*Je ne parle pas bien français*," she heard herself say, with the rolled "r" of her native tongue, and he replied it was no matter—just sitting there with her was communication enough.

After the interview, she packed her bag. There wasn't much to put in it, but that would soon be remedied. She carefully prepared a note for her parents, promising to be in touch as soon as she was established in the French capital. Stela got on the seven o'clock bus as usual for school the next morning and didn't return home.

Paris

October was drying the leaves in Paris and coloring them in quiet russets and yellows. Gusts of wind swept them to the sidewalks and gutters, and Claire buttoned her dark green trenchcoat to the top, folding in the left lapel. Carrying her black attaché case, she felt properly studious and purposeful, as she climbed the métro steps to the street and approached the massive Bibliothèque Nationale.

Her conversation the evening before with Philippe's parents was running through her mind. They were seated before thimble-sized glasses of burning *digestif*, which Claire still had to pretend to enjoy. His mother had on one of those box-cut Chanel suits you really imagine Frenchwomen of your mother's generation to wear and patent leather pumps on her fine-boned feet. "*Alors, Claire, vous êtes bien chez nous? Vous aimez Paris?* » Claire had launched into a heartfelt tirade on how Paris was the realization of a dream she'd barely been audacious enough to articulate. Its charm, its *caractère*, its culture, its bustle... Philippe's parents had beamed, two housecats lovingly stroked in the right direction. Claire was pleased to please. Philippe too, she noticed, was basking in the ambiance of genteel approval.

At the BN, she checked her case with Security, carrying her note-pad and purse into the vast reading room. At about five in the afternoon, she felt the need for a breath of air, and a cup of hot tea, in a neighboring café. Leaving the esplanade and descending the multitude of steps, she rounded the corner to the left of the huge building. She heard voices, a girl's, shrill, and a man's: an altercation. French people hurried by. Discreet or preoccupied, they barely glanced in the direction of the voices, but Claire held back, listening. Then she saw. A blue-uniformed policeman was demanding identity papers from a blond girl roughly her own age, possibly younger. The girl was dressed, despite the chilly weather, in a black miniskirt and a tight, black-and-silver top that left her midriff bare. Her legs, on the other hand, were swathed in tight-fitting boots that climbed to her knees. When she spoke, her French was disjointed, with "r's" like roller-coasters. The policeman was stern.

"*Vos papiers, mademoiselle.* You are not allowed to stay here. You are not allowed to solicit."

The blond girl argued and spat like a cat constrained. "I'm Italian, I tell you. Italian is European Community. I *have* the right!"

"Just show me your papers, then."

"My papers *chez moi*."

Claire watched while the policeman and a colleague, suddenly appearing out of nowhere, escorted the girl forcibly toward a squad car, guiding her firmly but not harshly.

Before she knew what had possessed her, Claire called out the first name that came to mind: "Maria! Maria! I'm here. What's going on? I'm so sorry I'm late for our appointment. I was waiting for you in front of the library." Claire posted herself squarely in front of the blond girl and the two French policmen, who looked her over—dark green raincoat, glasses, a bulging folder and a book in her hand--with mild astonishment. They relaxed the blond girl's elbows with a "*Désolé, mademoiselle,*" abandoning her to Claire.

Instead of running away, the girl looked curiously at Claire. "What is it to you?" she asked.

Claire didn't really know. "I…I hated to see you being pushed around by the police. Maybe, maybe," she stammered, "I really could offer you coffee or tea or something. I was just going to the café there for a break. I'm not from the police or anything. I'm doing some research at the Bibliothèque François Mitterrand." She looked at the book she was holding, then apologetically back at the young woman. For once she was glad of her accent, her hesitation in French. No one, not even this girl as foreign as herself, could take her for a French official of any sort.

The blond girl eyed her carefully. "All right. The name's not Maria, by the way. But it'll do."

"What's your name, then? I'm Claire."

The young woman said nothing. Claire couldn't quite decipher her expression: a mixutre of puzzled bemusement or a pliant form of defiance.

The girls entered the café, working their way toward a table in the back. Now that her initial impetus had subsided, Claire was thoroughly intimidated. Until this very minute, the only prostitutes she had approached were in books and their calling highly symbolic.

The blond girl positioned herself opposite Claire and spoke. "In another place, in another life, I had a name. I don't use it any more, though, and since I really *don't* have any papers—I mean, *they* kept them--no one has to know. Every working day, I make up a new one. That way it's someone else who gets *baisée* every time. Not me, not Stela."

The name had slipped out, and Claire caught it. Stela.

"*Mesdames?*"

Claire imagined the waiter was looking at them oddly. "*Deux cafés*," she said. "Will that be all right?" she asked her companion.

"Fine," Stela nodded. When the small, heavy cup was brought, she unwrapped two lumps of sugar and dropped them into the black liquid, stirred the syrupy mixture and held it to her lips. Her hands cradled the cup, imbibing its heat.

"I, uh… you don't want to…to do this work?" Claire couldn't imagine what the rules of small talk with streetwalkers might be. Beating around bushes had never much interested her anyway. People were always ready to tell you their truth, she'd discovered, if they felt sure you were listening.

"No. I was sold," Stela replied simply. "Twice."

"Sold? How could…?"

"A girl in my class at school. I don't know how much she made off the deal. I was betrayed by someone I knew. That's the worst. It's hard, having to face your own stupidity."

"And then…?"

"Then the Moldavian people-schleppers—my *own* people—sold me to my *mac*. He's an Albanian—they're the most violent, by the way, and here I am. Paris, City of Light. Land of *liberté, égalité, fraternité*. Destination of my dreams."

"Has it been long?"

"Since spring. First, they made me work in Italy. Basic training, you know? Listen, I'd better get back. *Merci* for the coffee."

Claire watched the silvery sheen of the girl's jersey and the pale skin of her back recede. That night, she begged Philippe to go through his law texts. What were the rules governing prostitution? What could be done to a prostitute? What could be done *for* one?

Philippe smiled at this sudden crusade but checked orders and decrees. Unlike in Belgium, little bargaining was possible. There, he told her, if you're brave enough, you denounce the network behind you in exchange for protection, legal asylum, and real working papers. Claire felt this ought to exist in France, had to exist. This girl, Stela, was a victim; the real culprits had to be taken to justice. Stela had to be helped.

Claire never expected to find herself face to face with her new acquaintance at the Louvre--not Stela in person, of course, but a gracious, wooden statue of Mary Magdalene, clothed in nothing more than the locks of her abundant hair. Claire had been ambling through the Renaissance galleries, and there was *La Madeleine*, striking a pose as a mystical ascetic, despite her scanty covering. The womanly saint clutched her arms around upper body, as if to hide her shame or ward off disrespectful looks. Claire saw her features marked by the same tragic hurt as the village girl from Moldavia.

In the Law of Moses, Claire knew, a prostitute was a sinner. Prostitution, sacred or otherwise, was a pagan practice and therefore proscribed. Yet hadn't a "sinner" woman anointed her Master's feet with the sweetest-smelling and most expensive unguent that could be bought? And hadn't he told his disciples that she had done a beautiful thing to him? A hazy idea half-formed in Claire's brain. After the Louvre, she stopped at a *parfumerie*.

The shelves of sparkling flacons glinted in the artifical light of the shop, row upon row. Claire studied the names: *Tabu, Ma Griffe, Opium, Lolita, Magie Noire, Obsession, Hypnotic Poison…* Nothing seemed right, least of all *poison hypnotique.* What about the classic, *Chanel Numéro Cinq*? It was expensive all right. The packaging was stark, the bottle strict and square-shouldered. Claire didn't want the *eau de toilette* but real *eau de parfum.* If a symbolic gesture was to be acted out, it had to be done properly. Claire handed over her international Visa card to the shopgirl, who wrapped the pricey bit of glass and pale liquid in a charming, miniature shopping bag of black velvet, with slim, golden ties.

At the Catholic church in her *quartier*, Claire knew that one pillar was decorated by a wooden icon in the Orthodox tradition, a solemn Christ Pantokrator, his right hand raised in blessing, while ring finger and thumb formed a perfect circle. At this time of the afternoon, the church would be open to the occasional worshiper. She slipped into the cool, shadowy sanctuary by the lateral oak door The massive, main one was kept locked. Claire approached the pillar and stared at the painting. The hieratic face was non-committal. Surreptitiously, she withdrew the bottle of Chanel Number Five from the depths of her bag, pressed the atomizer, and directed a thin spray of sweet drizzle onto the icon.

The heady, feminine scent reached her nostrils immediately. It's from Stela, she whispered. She can't do this, so I'm taking her place, that's all. It's from Stela and, as You can see, it is a beautiful thing.

༄

Claire went daily to the BN, but she didn't see the Moldavian girl again until after the lights and tinsel of Christmas had come down, and January rain made the city streets shine black and oily as early as five in the afternoon. They recognized each other at a glance, not far from the corner where they'd first crossed paths. With the familiarity of old acquaintances, they fell in step together, walking towards the café where they had first exchanged a few words.

Stela was wearing a plump, mauve *Gavroche* cap and her eyes were heavily outlined in dark brown kohl. The gray irises were like small pools of water in the depths of a well. They made Claire think of drowning.

"How are your studies?" the girl asked Claire, who wasn't expecting social amenities or conversation. "What is your subject?"

Afterward, she wished she had lied. She could have answered anything: ancient history, civilization… the choices were endless. But she had blurted out her topic. Sacred prostitution. How foolish she felt when the words were there; as if to this girl, betrayed, battered, exploited, the word "sacred" could come in the same breath as "prostitution."

Stela frowned. "Prostitution? You study prostitution?"

Claire tried to explain. No, she wasn't a law student, not a sociologist. It was something else; it was about ancient times, and symbolism, and…

Stela was frowning. "And you are succeeding in these studies?"

Claire thought back to her thesis advisor. "*Mademoiselle*, this topic has been abundantly developed. You must find a new angle, something more original…"

Claire had to shrug. "Not especially. There's so much to read. I haven't narrowed my research down enough yet. I have to write a paper. A big paper. It has to be original. I'm not sure what I want to say... On the other hand, since I met you, you know, in October, I have been looking into...into prostitution nowadays. Oh, I know—there's nothing symoblic about *that*." Claire floundered. She thought momentarily of the Chanel flacon at the bottom of her bag. It was time she came down to earth. "I wish there was something I could do to help you. I mean, help you get out of it, if that's what you want. I could go with you to an association. I've looked into it. There's *Le Nid*. They advise and harbor girls like you..."

"*They* will beat me if they find that out. And if they don't get their hands on me, they will get my family."

"Your family? But they're so far away."

"That's nothing, to *them*. They will hurt them and dishonor them. My parents are poor people but honest. They think I am a waitress here. Every week I phone them and tell them I am fine. I send money. These *macs*, they have all power. It is impossible to do anything against them. I can never go home, and I must never let myself get deported. They will always find me"

"But there must be something. I want to help you. What you have...it's not a life. It's inhuman."

"It is my punishment for dreaming."

"For dreaming?"

"Sometimes we think it is terrible when our dreams do not come true. Now, I can say, it is more terrible when they do."

The words stung like vipers. "Tell me what I can do for you then."

"You *really* want to help me?"

Claire nodded.

"And you want to write an original paper?"

Claire didn't reply to this. She couldn't imagine what Stela was thinking.

"So...you can take my place for some days. A little vacation for me, you see? And then you can write what you learn."

Claire wondered if the the girl were mocking her, but the flat, gray gaze was steady.

"Your hair is not so light as mine, but it's OK. I'll tell you what to do. *Quarante euros la pipe, cinquante la totale.* You don't need to memorize the dictionary. I'll give you my clothes, make-up. You can fit your hair into this cap. When my *mac* drives by to check, he'll think he's seeing me."

Claire was rigid, hanging onto her purse so tightly, her fingers ached.. She had imagined many things: going hand in hand with Stela to the police or to a charity office, putting her up at their own apartment (not that Philippe would be enthusiastic), driving her to Belgium or any other European country, even home… but this, never. To her shame, her mouth was completely dry. "I can't do it."

Stela's eyebrows lifted. "Why not? You say you will help me."

"Don't you see—that's not helping you. That's just making myself a victim, too. We'll be two victims instead of one…"

"Maybe prostitution is not a subject for you to study." Stela's voice was cold. Already, she was getting up from her seat.

"Please, Stela, please. I do want to do something for you, but not that."

"Where do you come from? You have never told me that."

"America. I come from America. "

"There are no whores in America, so you come to France?"

"No, no, that's not it. You see, I have a scholarship—that's money to study…" Why was she saying that, talking about money to this girl who had none, or none of her own? "There are special books here I need to see," she added lamely.

"You like it in Paris?"

"Yes." Her voice was small, abashed.

"Enjoy your stay." Stela snatched her coat and walked abruptly out of the café, bumping into a waiter on her way, not excusing herself, not turning back.

That evening, Claire told Philippe about her meeting with the Moldavian girl. She gathered some of her things to pack in a small suitcase—her jeans, but not the black pants suit. The novel she was reading, but not her research. She thought to stuff some post-cards of the City of Lights into her pocket. City of Lights, lights of illusion… She would place them in an album perhaps, but she would never send them. Finally, she removed from her purse the tiny, crystal bottle of expensive perfume and placed it in the far corner of her dresser.

Incense and good will accomplished no miracles, and she, Claire of the Congressional congratulations, could replace Stela no more in devotion than she could in debauchery. "Philippe?" She turned toward him as he sat reading. "I've always known people are not equal in the face of fortune, but in the face of dreams? I always imagined…" Her voice trailed off. She looked hard at him, willing him to understand.

He smiled at her over his law text, sphinxlike. "When you're back, we'll look into it. Legal recourse. Political pressure. Organizations. You can only take small steps, Claire. One thing at a time."

She knelt on the floor by him, resting her head for a moment in his lap. I'll return here, she mused, but when I say, "*moi,*" it will mean someone else.

Then she sat at her desk and wrote a letter to her thesis advisor. She was getting nowhere, she felt, and would like to discuss a complete change of focus, in a month or two, at his convenience. At present, she planned a visit to her home in the States. She needed time to think, she wrote. Rather a lot of time.

www.ingramcontent.com/pod-product-compliance
Ingram Content Group UK Ltd.
Pitfield, Milton Keynes, MK11 3LW, UK
UKHW040602210726
13854UKWH00008B/1715